TIMBER TOWN TALES

Stories and Images of Early Cadillac, Michigan (1871 to 1946)

by

CLIFF SJOGREN

COVER DESIGN BY PAMELA WELLIVER USING THE IMAGE OF THE SAWYERS SKETCHED BY CADILLAC ARTIST FRED H. LAMB, C. 1960'S.

THE LUMBER CAMP BY FRED H. LAMB

TIMBER TOWN TALES

by

CLIFF SJOGREN

FIRST EDITION - DECEMBER 2014
SECOND EDITION – NOVEMBER 2015

ISBN: 978-1-63192-489-7

CADILLAC PRINTING COMPANY, INC.

CADILLAC, MICHIGAN, USA

FOR FURTHER INFORMATION AND PURCHASES OF THIS PUBLICATION

YOU MAY CONTACT CADILLAC PRINTING COMPANY AT

(231) 775-2488

orders@cadillacprintingco.com

COPYRIGHT © CLIFF SJOGREN & WCHS

ALL PROFITS TO GO TO THE

WEXFORD COUNTY HISTORICAL SOCIETY & MUSEUM

WWW.WEXFORDCOUNTYHISTORY.ORG

DEDICATION

I dedicate this book to the countless 19th century pioneers who founded a community among the hills and tall pines on the eastern shore of a beautiful lake. The good work of those intelligent ladies and gentlemen, endowed with an admirable social conscience and a splendid work ethic, left generations of families since in deep appreciation of their contributions to our lives today.

Contents

Acknowledgements	vii
Introduction	ix
Big Trees and Big Hills	1
George Mitchell Had a Plan	4
Great Michigan Fire of 1871	7
Swedes Arrive in Clam Lake	10
Men and Women of Vision	13
Dr. Leeson And Tiger Oil	16
Health Care 1880's Style	19
Community Health Services Improve	23
The Villages of Wexford County	26
The Shay Locomotive Revolutionized An Industry	30
Camps, Jacks and Horses	34
The Icemen Came	37
Made in Cadillac	40
Timbers to Taters	43
Rural Schools of Wexford County	46
Cadillac High School	49
The Michigan Wildcat	52
The Ladies Wanted A Library	55
Boys Behaving Badly	58
They Oughta Make A Movie	61
Saboteurs and Toasters	64
Ballots and Ordinances	67
Cadillac Reinvents Itself	70
Religion Was A Priority	73
Fire Was An Ever Present Danger	76

Contents, continued

A Tough And Forgiving Lake	79
The Yanks Are Coming	82
Motor City North	85
The 1920's Was An Era Of Change	88
A Vacation Destination, Part One	91
A Vacation Destination, Part Two	94
Living And Giving During The Great Depression	98
The Civilian Conservation Corps	101
The Works Progress Administration	104
A Child Of The Great Depression	108
Discipline During the Times of Turmoil	112
Leaders And Followers	115
Wexford County Goes To War	118

ACKNOWLEDGEMENTS

If not for my hometown newspaper with its longtime commitment to keeping the Cadillac area history in the minds of its readers, this book would not have happened. The Huckle family has owned the Cadillac News (formerly the Cadillac Evening News) since 1926. They not only consolidated our area's colorful history into two celebratory issues published in 1951 and 1971 (see Introduction) but also ran my 38 stories with photographs weekly during 2014 that were created primarily from those special editions. I particularly want to express my appreciation to Cadillac News Editor Matthew Seward for his encouragement, efficiency, and good editing.

    I thank Pamela Welliver of the Cadillac Printing Company for assembling all of the parts of this book and adding valuable suggestions on design and organization. Nan Taylor provided much guidance along the way as well.

    When Tom Taylor happened to attend a Wexford County Historical Society Board meeting, the enthusiasm for the book shown by the members motivated him to launch a successful fund raising initiative. Several unselfish members of the community provided the essential financial support for the first edition.

    Finally, Jack Westman, who was the first one to tell me that, "You need to do a book!" is a 1945 Cadillac High School graduate and Professor Emeritus, University of Wisconsin School of Medicine and Public Health. Jack was the major donor to the museum's initiative to have the 216 pages of those two Cadillac Evening News editions digitized, cleaned, de-acidified, and bound for public viewing. Jack and his CHS classmate and friend, Ed Leutzinger, provided me with many ideas and much support as I transported my Cadillac News stories to "Timber Town Tales."

CS

MAIN STREET – CADILLAC, MICHIGAN
SKETCH BY FRED H. LAMB

INTRODUCTION

The Cadillac area has a rich and interesting history. Other than Judge William R. Peterson's well-researched book of the community's earliest years, "The View from Courthouse Hill," Debra Bricault's "Cadillac: Vintage Postcard Memories," and essays on local history featured in the Cadillac News, not much has been published for public perusal. That void has been addressed in this book.

"Timber Town Tales" is a gathering of interesting snippets from a number of mostly Pre-World War II sources consisting of books, newspapers, photographs, and the author's personal life experiences. The most important of those sources are two celebratory issues of the Cadillac Evening News: The 96-page June 6, 1951 "Golden Anniversary" issue (a copy retained by my wife, Patricia Chick Sjogren, a member of the staff that created that edition) and the 116-page June and July 1971 "Cadillac Centennial" issues (a copy retained by my father because his father was a 19th and early 20th century Cobbs and Mitchell employee in Cadillac and Jennings.)

Other major sources are the "Cadillac City Directory, 1900," by Willard A. Norton (unabridged version,) 1900, 235 pp.; "A History of Northern Michigan and Its People," by Perry F. Powers, 1912, 562 pp., and, "History of Wexford County Michigan," by John H. Wheeler, 1903, 641 pp. Except for the Judge Peterson and Deb Bricault books the sources listed above have been digitized and are accessible on the Wexford County Historical Society Website at www.wexfordcountyhistory.org

The title was carefully chosen. Because most of the story lines were taken from secondary sources where features described in two or more accounts of a happening were occasionally though rarely in conflict with each other, one might find it inappropriate to include the term "history" in the title. The reader will, however, gain a sense of the Cadillac area culture as well as a general picture of the remarkable number and the high quality of accomplishments during its first 75 years of existence.

A wilderness was tamed and an industrial powerhouse emerged that attracted the attention of a nation.

Honorable and benevolent men and women who cared deeply about their new community and its citizens planted the seeds and nurtured them into the fine place to live, work, and play that countless residents and visitors continue to enjoy today.

All money generated by "Timber Town Tales" sales beyond printing and mailing costs will be donated to the Wexford County Historical Society and Museum. Your contribution will help us both preserve and display for public viewing and research our remarkable collection of historically important artifacts and documents.

CS

CANAL BETWEEN LAKES MITCHELL AND CADILLAC
SKETCH BY FRED H. LAMB

Wexford County, Michigan

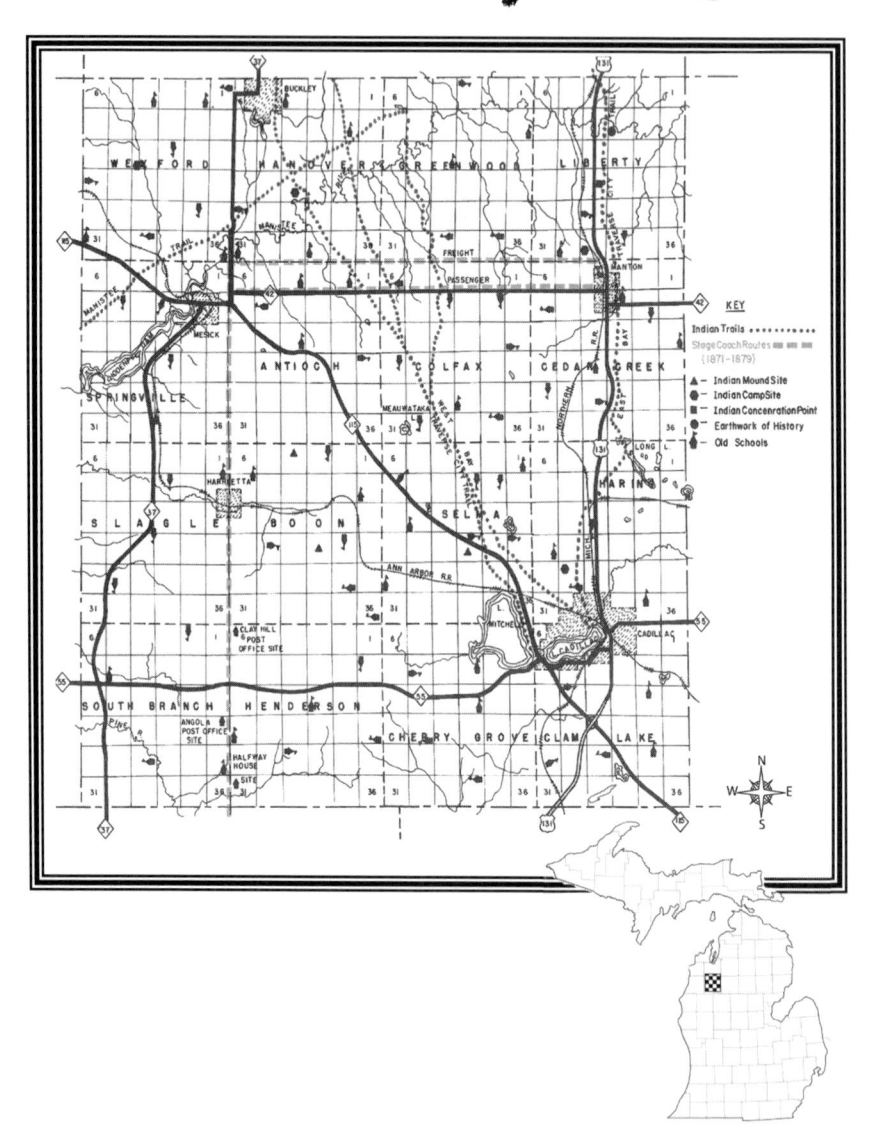

TIMBER TOWN TALES

BIG TREES AND BIG HILLS

Teams of horses haul large logs to the water or rail for transport to the mills.

Wexford County was first settled in the mid-1860s by a small group of New York families who established the Manistee River community of Sherman in the northwestern part of the county. J. H. Wheeler, one of Sherman's pioneers, wrote about the area's history in his well-researched book, "History of Wexford County, Michigan," (1903.) When Wheeler asked Perry Hannah, a leading citizen of Traverse City, to provide his impressions of the wilderness territory, Hannah's written reply included this description of his walk through Wexford County in January 1854.

TIMBER TOWN TALES

"There was not a single sign of a trail of any kind to travel by, which compelled us to constantly use our compass, as very little sunshine can be seen at that season of the year beneath the thick timber that then shrouded the whole country. This was the most tedious journey I ever experienced in the early days of Grand Traverse."

Further in his letter Hannah penned the following about engaging "a hardy old pioneer and hunter" in 1857 to survey Wexford County to determine the feasibility of creating a more direct carriage route to Grand Rapids. Hannah writes of his aide's report.

"First rate; it could not be better. I tell you, Mr. Hannah, if we get a settler through to Grand Traverse on that line we will be sure of him. By golly! them hills, they be awful big, and they all slope this way, and the settler that gets here will never go back over those hills."

That carriage route was not to be for many years. Wexford County remained, as one writer opined, "an untamed wilderness of wolves, swamps, and high hills." The towering eastern white pines remained in place, casting their unbroken shade over the forest floor until a timber seeker from Indiana arrived on the eastern shore of Little Clam Lake in late 1870.

Every once in awhile an individual comes along who has the wisdom, the skills, and the compassion to create a vibrant living and work environment for the greater community. George A. Mitchell, founder of Clam Lake (Cadillac) in 1871, was such a man.

When Mitchell arrived on the eastern shore of Little Clam Lake (Lake Cadillac) in 1870, he found himself in an area that had been by-passed by tree harvesters. Neither rail service nor a large river was available to bring the cut timbers to the mills. At that time, the timber industry was increasing dramatically in Michigan producing construction lumber and wood products to serve a rapidly growing immigrant population. Combining his dream with a good plan, Mitchell built a town that would soon become an economic powerhouse.

Although there were no known permanent settlers in the immediate Little Clam Lake area at that time, records reveal that in 1869 James Whaley established his successful farm six or seven miles from the lake near the southeast corner of the county.

TIMBER TOWN TALES

GEORGE MITCHELL HAD A PLAN

George Mitchell, Founder of Cadillac in 1871

TIMBER TOWN TALES

George A. Mitchell was born on a farm in New York in 1824, the last of Charles and Lydia's 12 children. His grandfather was a Revolutionary War hero. In 1861, George moved to Kendallville, Indiana, a community founded by his brother, William. George enlisted in the Union Army during the Civil War where his business acumen was soon recognized. While stationed mostly in southern war zones, he quickly rose to the rank of Lieutenant Colonel responsible for the distribution of millions of dollars to troops and support staffs.

After the war, Mitchell became a timber-seeker with a plan. He knew that the Grand Rapids and Indiana Railroad (G. R. & I. RR) would soon reach Wexford County. With rail service, he could transport his harvested logs to mills and his manufactured products to consumers. He observed that Little Clam Lake with its seven-mile shoreline was connected by a half–mile stream with Big Clam Lake with a ten and one-half-mile shoreline. He also knew that, except for a few small hills where he planned to build his community, the flat terrain surrounding the lakes was ideal to transport logs short distances to the water's edge on horse-drawn sleds. The lakes' waters, supplied primarily by the vast pine dominated wetlands that surround both lakes, flow easterly to the Clam River outlet at present day Cadillac. Taking advantage of prevailing westerly winds and the natural water flow would make it relatively easy to float the cut logs to the village mills and rail service.

An important element of Mitchell's plan was the re-routing of the G. R. & I. RR line. The rail company designed the route to run between Little Clam Lake and Big Clam Lake, the most direct line to Charlevoix and Petoskey. But Mitchell, aided by his family's influence with the G. R. & I. RR, convinced the company to veer east and lay their tracks near the eastern shore of Little Clam Lake. (Today's maps show that both the White Pine Trail, constructed on the G. R. & I. rail bed and US-131 Highway, display a north-eastward turn a few miles south of Cadillac.)

TIMBER TOWN TALES

Soon after he arrived in 1871, Mitchell's plan was applied. So magnetic was his allure that in less than one year his new community numbered 125 families and dozens of business operations, including timber camps, sawmills, builders, and shops to serve a rapidly growing population. Managing the new enterprises and public services were a group of intelligent and hard working folks who embraced Mitchell's plan, made a lot of money, invested heavily in their new community, and guided the tiny village on its way to prosperity.

What Mitchell did not know was that a catastrophic event loomed that would place an urgency on the full implementation of his plan.

TIMBER TOWN TALES

GREAT MICHIGAN FIRE OF 1871

The Great Fires of 1871 created an opportunity for George Mitchell and other lumber producers. This is a photo of the Harris Mill, 1872.

When George Mitchell arrived in Clam Lake (Cadillac) he would not know that a catastrophic event would soon cause him to plat his community, harvest some trees, and get the mills operating quickly.

On October 8, the Great Michigan Fire of 1871 unleashed its destructive force on a hundred-mile wide swath through central Lower Michigan from Port Huron and Saginaw on Lake Huron to Holland and Manistee on Lake Michigan.

An unusually dry summer was followed by the "perfect storm" of lightning and very strong winds. Dozens of fires were ignited by the lightning and fueled by the slash from cuttings in timber harvest areas and the stacks of dried lumber stored at the mills. Manistee was among the many communities that were severely damaged or destroyed. Wexford County was left mostly undamaged.

It was also the date of the Peshtigo fire in Wisconsin and the Great Chicago Fire. Some were convinced but failed to prove that the fires were caused by a widespread meteor shower.

Those disastrous fires propelled the tiny village of Clam Lake on its way to becoming a major timber harvest and wood product-manufacturing center. The Michigan and Wisconsin fire-ravaged mills were unable to produce the construction lumber that was sorely needed to build new homes for immigrants and rebuild structures destroyed by the fires.

Mitchell now faced a formidable challenge; organize a community and accelerate tree harvesting and wood products manufacturing to address a serious societal need.

As early as the summer of 1871 logs had been floated to the village and planing and saw mills were in operation along the eastern shore of Little Clam Lake. A railroad crew's lodging facility was converted into a crude hotel for men who arrived to work in the forests and mills. (It has been written that the first "business" in the new settlement was a keg of whiskey set on a stump near the rail crew's bunkhouse.) Most of the early downtown businesses were located along West Mason Street.

Mitchell recruited experienced timber managers and workers who became both his close friends and his noteworthy competitors. Jonathon Cobbs, who built his mill at the southeast corner of the lake, would soon merge with the Mitchells to form the giant Cobbs & Mitchell enterprise and become one of the largest wood product manufacturing companies in Michigan.

New arrivals came pouring into the village where they soon found well-paying jobs during that nation-wide troubled economic period. They consisted mostly of recently landed Swedes, who later became the largest ethnic group, Canadians, and Americans from New York, New England, Ohio, Illinois, and Indiana.

Soon after the Great Michigan Fire, the Village of Clam Lake emerged as a rapid-growth tree harvest and processing center that attracted the attention of a nation.

TIMBER TOWN TALES

SWEDES ARRIVE IN CLAM LAKE

Cadillac – Swedish Baptist – Sunday School Class – year ?

Back row – L to R....Mildred Ogren, Esther Erickson, Myrtle Grandin, Sylvia Nesberg, Esther Olson

Center – Sunday School teacher – Emily Neal

Front row – L to R...Hilma Olson, Ella Carlson, Mable Lundquist, Esther Lundin, Gurley M. Hammar

Swedes constituted the largest immigrant group during the late 19th Century.

When I mentioned to my Swedish seatmate during a flight to Stockholm several years ago that my grandparents emigrated from Sweden in the late 19th century he responded with, "They must have been very intelligent and very courageous."

10

TIMBER TOWN TALES

Entirely willing to accept his generalization, I asked him to explain. With a smile, he answered, "They were smart enough to leave Sweden and brave enough to go where few spoke their language."

He said that at that time, both the state and the church were overly intrusive into the lives of the freedom-loving Swedes. Further, Europe was experiencing a major recession and many mostly young men sought a new life in North America.

Swedish immigrants began arriving in Clam Lake in 1872. They brought with them their well-developed skills in tree harvesting and wood product manufacturing. They introduced new tools and improved ways to move large timbers to the mills. They were accustomed to hard and dangerous working conditions in a cold climate with shortened winter daylight hours.

By the mid-1880s, Cadillac had three Swedish churches, the Swedish Evangelical Mission, Swedish Baptist, and Emmanuel Lutheran. All services were conducted in their native tongue until well into the 20th century and some until the 1930s.

In 1873, the Presbyterians invited the Evangelical Mission members to conduct services in their church twice on Christmas Day. The churches and homes of most Swedes were in the near northeast section of town between East Pine and River streets. There were three Swedish language newspapers.

The 1900 Cadillac census lists about 80 family entries for the surname "Johnson" and nearly 50 each for "Anderson" and "Peterson."

The town's leadership recognized the Swedish contributions to their new community by labeling the high school athletic teams the "Vikings" and selecting the Swedish flag colors of yellow and blue as their school colors.

In neighboring Tustin, a Michigan Historic Site sign, "Unto a New Land," includes in part, "Swedish immigrants, anxious to escape famine and an unsympathetic government, flowed into the Midwest frontier of America from the 1870s to 1890s searching for land and work. Railroads and lumbering industries offered attractive opportunities to these immigrants. The Grand Rapids & Indiana Railroad sent the Rev. J.P. Tustin to Sweden to recruit laborers for construction of its line. As an inducement, the railroad donated eighty acres to the Swedish colony of New Blekinge (Tustin). Swedes swarmed to this vicinity building the railroad, logging the forest and laboring in sawmills."

One way to get a general sense of the ethnic distribution in early Cadillac is to examine Mercy Hospital admission statistics. In a 1909 report published by the hospital entitled "Nativity of Patients" (country of birth,) the numbers of Swedish natives were followed in numerical order by natives of Canada, Germany, Holland, Norway, Ireland, Finland, Denmark, and England. These data suggest that Cadillac depended heavily on northern European immigrants during the first few decades of its existence.

TIMBER TOWN TALES

MEN AND WOMEN OF VISION

The Diggins family home on the NE corner of Shelby and Harris streets was razed in the 1940s for construction of a telephone company office building.

The words, "Cadillac: City of Quality Made Possible by Men of Vision" appeared on the upper front-page banner of the Cadillac Evening News during the early and mid-Twentieth Century. That statement properly defined our area's early settlers.

Many of those industrial, business, and civic leaders became very rich and chose to live and invest unselfishly in their new community. A few made substantial gifts to their town.

George Mitchell, along with his nephews, William and Austin Mitchell, set a standard of benevolence that was embraced by many of their colleagues. The Mitchells

TIMBER TOWN TALES

designed the community and substantially supported the construction of the infrastructure and buildings to make it a pleasant work and living environment.

A full square block near the central business district was set aside for a school. School buildings and playground facilities were heavily subsidized. Religious groups were given land on which to build their churches. Roadways were soon constructed. Land was gifted for the cemetery at the village's south entrance and for parklands between the lakes and on the north shore of Little Clam Lake.

The main north / south street (Mitchell Street today) was constructed with adequate width to allow horse-drawn carts laden with timbers to turn around handily. (Did George know that a five-lane street would be much appreciated by future generations?)

The Mitchell family accumulated and invested much of their wealth in their town. On Aug. 8, 1878, soon after the village George Mitchell founded became the City of Cadillac, he died from a carriage accident near his home.

Another major benefactor of the period was the Delos F. Diggins family. Delos and his wife, Esther Gerrish Diggins, funded the construction of Mercy Hospital and purchased the equipment needed to begin serving the patients. The Diggins family also arranged for the hospital's association with the Sisters of Mercy of Big Rapids.

Delos died shortly before the hospital opened in 1908. Esther carried on the family's commitment to their community in 1912 by funding the two three-story wings of Cadillac High School, which more than doubled the floor space of the structure.

Upon Esther's death in 1916, her estate left Mercy Hospital an additional $10,000. Their beautiful home on the northeast corner of Shelby and East Harris streets was razed in 1947 for the construction of a telephone company building.

The forest and mill workers were well treated by the companies. On a September Saturday in 1888, the

TIMBER TOWN TALES

Cummer Company closed all operations and hosted their workers for a picnic. A special Grand Rapids & Indiana RR train left Cadillac at 6 a.m. for Petoskey, Bay View, and Harbor Springs with 605 company workers, returning at 11 p.m. that evening.

Among influential men who left their mark on our history in the tree harvest and wood products business were, Jacob Cummer and son, Wellington; Jonathon W. Cobbs and son, Frank; brothers, Charles E. and Elbert J. Haynes; William L. Saunders; brothers, George F., Walter S., and Albert E. Williams; Henry LaBar; Jacob Cornwell; brothers, Henry H. and O. L. Harris; and many others. (Fortunately, there were no Bernie Madoffs among those noble citizens.)

Biographies of most of these men are included in John H. Wheeler's book, "History of Wexford County, Michigan," accessible by a link on the Wexford County Historical Society and Museum Website at wexfordcountyhistory.org

DR. LEESON AND TIGER OIL

Photo from an ad submitted by Dr. Leeson to the abridged edition of the "Cadillac City Directory, 1900," W. A. Norton, Compiler and publisher, 1900.

TIMBER TOWN TALES

It was once said that Dr. John Leeson, Clam Lake's first medical doctor, would work with "drawn curtains in deep mysterious seclusion to compound the healing mixtures whose power and euphonious names have become so widely known." The colorful doctor, famous for his signature creation, Tiger Oil, an elixir "Good for man or beast" arrived in the village in April 1872. His office was located on Beech Street.

In 1851, at age 16, the young man left his native England and settled in Ontario. He became interested in medicine by watching his father treat sheep, horses and cattle. As a teenager, he created his first medicine and soon after made, in his words, "medicines for my friends and for stock as well as performing some minor surgery."

Before entering the medical field, he toiled on farms, managed a bakery in Chicago, and taught school. After some months in Ann Arbor "under a doctor's guidance," he enrolled in the Detroit Medical College from where he graduated in 1869. Before arriving in Clam Lake, he practiced his profession in Manistee.

Dr. Leeson began crafting his new medicines with what he termed as "three articles" that most likely were never identified for the public. Six years later he had created a compound of 26 "articles" that he labeled Tiger Oil, which, according to his words, "challenges an equal for its merits for the relief or cure of diseases generally."

He advertised that his Tiger Oil would cure coughs, colds, neuralgia, toothache, rheumatism, fainting, Globus, hystericus, spinal meningitis, fits, flux, diarrhea, dysentery, cholera, diphtheria, colic, and more. It can also be used for sprains, cuts, burns, and stiffness of joints. "For ox or horse," the good doctor suggests, "use ten times as much as for man in similar diseases, for other animals in proportion to size."

Dr. Leeson also made medicines for special diseases under such labels as Elephant of the Blood, Lion Lung Lotus, Best Bitters, Sea Seal Salve, Head Have Hair, Hands Heal Handy, and Monitor Liver and Laxative Pills, all of which "are guaranteed to do their work effectually."

It had been reported that by January 1874, Dr. Leeson had treated 1,026 patients without losing one. The elixir was distributed throughout the U.S. and in a few other countries.

His daughter, Ethelyn, was the first non-Native American born in Clam Lake. When Dr. Leeson died at age 87 in 1922, his secret formula became the property of Russell Gold, a Cadillac pharmacist. Gold indicated that he made Tiger Oil by the gallon while the doctor had made it by the barrel.

Reading about the doctor's illustrative professional life leaves one wondering about the composition of his many secretive medicines. Was he an accomplished scientist who uncovered some of the mysteries of drugs for healing? Or had he discovered early on the powers of the placebo effect as a cure for our ailments? We may never know!

HEALTH CARE 1880'S STYLE

The Dr. John Leeson Building located on the southeast corner of Beech and Mitchell streets (c.1890.)

The scene: *Injured logger Sven Johnson is transported in a horse-drawn wagon from the camp to Doctor Sawbones' in-home office on East Cass Street. While Sven awaits the doctor he reads the following information on the waiting room sign:*

FEES FOR SERVICES OF SEVEN LOCAL PHYSICIANS. Vaccinations, 75¢; prescriptions, $1; day / night home visits, $1 / $2; anesthesia, $5; obstetrics, $10; tonsil removal, $15 - $25; craniotomy, $25; amputations, finger, $5 - $10; leg, $25 - $50; hip $100- $200' (and more.)

TIMBER TOWN TALES

Doctor: Your leg will need to be amputated, Sven.
Sven: How much will it cost?
Doctor: $30 plus $5 if you want anesthesia. Are you able to pay?
Sven: No.
Doctor: Don't worry. I will ask Mr. Mitchell to help. After the surgery my wife will take you home in our buggy.

Legendary Doctor John Leeson, highlighted in an earlier story, and two additional physicians set up medical practices within months after the 1871 arrival of Clam Lake's founder George Mitchell.

The following winter, Mitchell agreed to purchase clothing for poor children. Payments from community funds were issued to needy citizens for doctor bills, burials and coffins. Rising communities in those days had to find ways of taking care of their sick and needy quickly. Those who were able to pay for medical services did so or Dr. Leeson would have their names printed in the newspaper.

Because Cadillac did not have a hospital, most patients were treated in their home, the doctor's home office, or his downtown office. Dr. I. N. Coleman leased rooms at the American House Hotel on the southeast corner of East Harris and Mitchell streets. There he had appliances of "therapeutic" value and electricity to treat most diseases and injuries. Some patients were sent to a medical facility in Big Rapids.

A major health issue was the unregulated movement of domesticated animals on village streets. Finally, in June 1877, the Village Council acted to prohibit horses, mules, cattle, swine and geese from roaming loose in the community.

In 1883, the health board chairman was asked to have the "filth and garbage removed from our alleys and byways and privies should be disinfected." If not done, "then disease must run its course among the rich and poor." A request was also made that funeral services for those who died from contagious diseases be brief and attended by as few as possible.

An 1885 sanitation ordinance required that private drains or sewers, privies, tubs and holding tanks had to be cleaned regularly and the waste moved in sealed containers to "outside of the city limits." Men known as "scavengers," who were required to be licensed by the city, were hired to dispose of the waste materials. (I presume most city residents chose to enjoy their picnics within the city limits!)

Another hazard of the period was the effect that sudden loud noises had on animals. Railroad and factory whistles and barking dogs would frighten teams of horses and oxen often causing a "run away." Drivers would be thrown from their loaded wagons and pedestrians injured as the animals instinctively headed in haste for their yards.

Willie Hodgkins, a small boy, was bitten by a dog and fell ill with hydrophobia (rabies.) A cow bitten by the same dog died. Mayor pro-tem Cummer soon issued a proclamation ordering that all un-muzzled dogs be shot. Willie had not been expected to live, but the next month he was on the streets again. Because of his weakened condition and uncontrollable fits, money was raised in the community to send him to an asylum.

As early as 1877 some serious social issues were raised through the initiatives of a group of ladies who launched the Temperance Christian Union. In 1887, the TCU released the following statement: "Horrors to which drink exposes women are worse than those of slavery. The sufferings of the wives and daughters of drinking men are more acute and constant than most men are probably capable of experiencing. We all know this, yet we go calmly in the old way as if we either thought women ought to be abused or believed that though the matter was pitiful, no help could be found for it."

One February day Mr. R. E. Corneil died soon after being severely injured by a rolling log on a forest skid way. It was then written that "... his soul took its flight from earth and left the mortal tenement for which but a few days before he had been a model of manly vigor." Today we would simply say that he had "died unexpectedly." While more efficiently worded today, it is much less colorful.

Community Health Services Improve

Mercy Hospital, funded by the Delos Diggins family, was constructed in 1907. This scene was captured around 1911.

It was written that in 1888 Dr. Hutchinson made a patient's visit to his dental office a "positive luxury" because his new operating chair was so "ingeniously arranged and so admirably adapted."

It was supposed that anyone with an "average degree of curiosity" would willingly have his teeth removed by the dentist "to feel and witness the possible evolutions and contortions of that wonderful chair."

In April 1893, Dr. G. Brown installed an approved gas procedure for the "painless extraction of teeth."

A female doctor served Wexford County as early as 1889. Mrs. (so titled in the article) E. C. Dayhuff established her practice near Meauwataka.

TIMBER TOWN TALES

In July 1889 a new city dumpsite was created adjacent to the northeast side of Maple Hill Cemetery. The dump's location destroyed the fish habitat of two nearby ponds. That site existed at least through the mid-1940s providing a nice venue for shooting rats with 22-caliber rifles.

Several serious diseases were treated during the late eighteenth and early nineteenth centuries. In February 1876, Manton reported a number of chicken pox cases. The 2-year-old daughter of the William Saunders family died of cholera infantum in August 1891.

An outbreak of scarlet fever in October 1893 led to several deaths and schools were closed through most of the month.

A smallpox epidemic was reported in a Hoxeyville lumber camp and in Manton in 1908. A more widespread distribution of the disease in 1939 was reported.

Typhoid fever arrived in Cadillac in August 1921. A clinic was created for free inoculations and a doctor was sent by the state.

From the beginning, water quality was a primary issue for the community's leadership. During the fall of 1892, a large water main was completed that extended from the new water works facility provided by the Cummer Corporation to a tower on Diggins Hill.

Because of the many large pine stumps encountered during the project, tunnels beneath those obstructions were dug. The scene was colorfully described as "... monstrous stumps standing over it (the pipe) like stalwart sentinels until the march of improvement in that direction demands their removal."

The Cadillac Water Company installed powerful Worthington pumps that were able to deliver 3 million gallons of water per day. To draw water for the residents, a 475-foot filtered pipe reaching a depth of 19 feet was installed in the northeast corner of the lake in December 1892. The following summer dead fish and nine barrels of dead lizards were washed ashore on Little Clam Lake (Lake Cadillac.)

TIMBER TOWN TALES

In July 1928 a special committee recommended wells as the primary community water source, although lake water seemed to be favored by most users. In a referendum conducted the following September, users preferred the lake water by a four to one majority.

Even though money flowed freely in the new city, there were occasional suicide deaths caused by business failures.

When John G. Mosser, one of Cadillac's pioneer builders of homes and commercial properties, experienced financial difficulties in 1893, he assigned his business interests to E. F. Sawyer "for the benefit of his creditors." Soon after, Mosser's wife received from her husband a small package with a note from Niagara Falls indicating that he would "bid goodbye to the world that evening at 4:00." The thoughtfulness and preparation that preceded his suicide is noteworthy.

Mercy Hospital, built in 1907 as a gift from the Delos Diggins family, has since provided up-to-date medical services to the residents of Wexford, Missaukee, and Osceola counties. In 1938, the hospital leased the former Diggins home, a grand structure located on the northeast corner of Shelby and East Harris streets, for a school to train nurses.

In May 1944 the hospital was told they would receive a supply of penicillin, the "wonder drug" created and successfully used to treat injured and ill military personnel during World War II.

In 1946, ground was broken for a three-story addition to Mercy Hospital that would add 84 beds and in 1965 the hospital added an image intensifier for the X-ray department, the first of its kind north of Grand Rapids.

The schoolchildren of Cadillac protested the school board's decision to reduce the morning recess time from 15 to three minutes in 1887. A petition signed by "every scholar affected" led to the reinstatement of the 15-minute period. One might wonder what the students would do if geometry classes were reduced to three minutes.

TIMBER TOWN TALES

THE VILLAGES OF WEXFORD COUNTY

This view of Main Street in Manton shows the J. Berry Meat Market on the left, c. late 1800s.

Wexford County's first European-descendant settler was Benjamin W. Hall who in 1862 built his cabin at the Manistee River near present day Sherman.
 The community, settled by New Yorkers, became the first county seat. A courthouse, hotel, sawmills, and several shops and homes were soon constructed. The county's first newspaper, the Pioneer, was launched in Sherman.
 Because its location was near the river and the Newaygo Trail (Leelanau County to Grand Rapids) the tiny settlement was destined to become an important business center.

TIMBER TOWN TALES

Hopes were soon dashed, however, when George A. Mitchell founded the Village of Clam Lake in 1871 at the opposite corner of the county. The new settlement sprung to life when the Grand Rapids and Indiana Railroad (G.R. & I. RR) arrived on the eastern shore of Little Clam Lake (Lake Cadillac.)

The sequence of new Wexford County settlements was easily predictable. Because trains provided the primary transport of people, supplies, raw materials and manufactured products, settlements were founded and flourished along rail lines. Clam Lake was platted in 1872 and Manton was platted in 1874 as the G.R. & I. RR made its way north.

Soon after merchants, Ezra Harger and George Manton, built their businesses in Manton, a sawmill and school were erected. Religious services were held in the railroad depot.

By the end of the century, Manton's factories produced staves and headings (barrels,) last blocks (molds for making shoes,) and seed planters. The Manton Produce Company had a grain elevator, a mill for grinding feed, and storage for 10,000 bushels of grain.

The Village of Manton was Wexford County's only community besides Cadillac to eventually be designated a "city."

The Toledo, Ann Arbor, and Northern Michigan Railway reached Cadillac on January 1, 1887. The railroad was then extended diagonally across Wexford County on to its terminus at Frankfort on Lake Michigan. The communities through which it passed provided the primary financial support for the railroad construction. Boon, Harrietta, Yuma and Mesick owe their existence to the railway.

The Village of Boon was platted in 1889 and soon had two sawmills and a bowl factory.

Frank Gaston founded Harriette, later Harrietta, in 1889. A sawmill was established to harvest hardwoods that were used by local manufacturers to make "novelties." Soon after, the economy was strengthened by the manufacture of stoves, bricks, shingles and wood alcohol. A state-managed fish hatchery, one of the first in Michigan, was erected in 1901 at near-by Slagle Creek, a fine trout stream.

Harrietta was incorporated in 1891 under the name of Gaston, but quickly returned to its original name under pressure from the Ann Arbor Railroad. In 1892, Harrietta became only the second place in the U.S. to manufacture alcohol and acetate of lime by combining smoke from the charcoal kilns with steam generated by cold water over copper coils that was then condensed into a liquid.

The coal kilns and the chemical plant in Harrietta were transferred to the Village of Yuma, platted in 1893. Trees in the Yuma area had not yet been harvested. To reduce transport costs it was decided "that (it) would be cheaper to move the plant to the timber than the timber to the plant." Seven cars of charcoal each day were being shipped from Yuma and Harrietta. After the wood was depleted, Yuma turned to agriculture for its livelihood.

The Village of Mesick was platted in 1890 soon after the arrival of the Ann Arbor Railroad. A sawmill and a handle factory were established. The Williams Brothers owned a last-block factory that was moved to Cadillac during the 1890s. A two-and-a-half-mile rail spur connecting Sherman with Mesick was built which led to increased business activity in Mesick while Sherman's economic strength declined precipitously.

Between 1870 and 1900, at least 35 settlements, mostly with post offices and schools, were scattered throughout Wexford County. Nearly all were either alongside the two major rail lines or one of the many spurs served primarily by timber company-owned Shay locomotives that made their way deep into area forests on 36 gauge (inch) rails.

While only a few of those communities exist today, many of those early locations are familiar among local residents. They include Angola, Axin, Bagnall, Bandola, Baxter, Benson, Bunyea, Colfax, Coline, Cornel, Eleanor, Elton, Farnsworth, Gilbert, Glengary, Greenwood, Haire,

TIMBER TOWN TALES

Hooper's Switch, Hoxeyville, Meauwataka, Millersville, Miner's Rollway, Mystic, Putman's Siding, Rodingen, Root's Mill, Six Corners, Soper, Springdale, Stocking, Summit, Thorp's Corners, Viola, Walls and Wheatland.

During that period virtually all of the communities of the county were founded as timber harvest and processing centers.

THE SHAY LOCOMOTIVE REVOLUTIONIZED AN INDUSTRY

Mitchell Brother's 1887 Shay Locomotive taking timber to the company's extensive facilities at Jennings, northeast of Cadillac.

Early Cadillac was well served by its industrial pioneers. Family names such as Mitchell, Cummer, Diggins, and Cobbs would bring to mind intelligent, innovative men with a strong sense of community and a "can do" mentality. Ephraim Shay, inventor of a highly specialized locomotive, was a multi-talented, well-read man who most certainly deserves a place among that distinguished group.

Timber seekers knew that Wexford County had some of the best stands of white pine in Northern Michigan. They were also aware of the challenge they would face transporting the felled logs to the mills. Horse-drawn sleds loaded with timbers would experience problems navigating a Wexford County terrain characterized by many hills and wetlands. Seldom were the sleds used for the transport of logs more than one or two miles.

In 1877, Shay arrived in Cadillac from his home in Ohio with an idea. He built a sawmill about two miles north of Cadillac near the Grand Rapids and Indiana Railroad (G. R. & I RR) and laid down about two miles of rail. He then described to local machinist William Crippen his plan for the creation of a special locomotive that could penetrate the forest and bring logs to the mills.

Shay's plan required a specified combination of structural and propulsion devices, mostly invented by others, to build his locomotive at Crippen's machine shop located on the west end of West Bremer Street. With its vertical boiler, the steam-powered engine was designed to direct power to all 12 wheels. The drive shaft featured universal joints that allowed for "bends" that enabled the locomotive to ride through sharp turns, grade changes, and uneven terrain and rail tracks. The six wheels on the right side of the locomotive were gear-driven.

(All of the mechanical features mentioned here, and more, can be seen on the Shay locomotive built in 1898 and on display in Cadillac's City Park.)

This low maintenance locomotive was not designed for speed, as its cruising speed was between eight and ten miles per hour. Few things could go wrong with the locomotive that could not be fixed at the harvest site. If more track was needed, workers would make it out of hardwood found around the cutting area.

The Shay locomotive revolutionized the timber industry. On its 36-gauge track, the Shay was able to glide through the forests with ease. Woodcuttings along the way were gathered to fuel the steam-driven engines. The locomotives had the power to tow up to 40 cars (rail wagons) that averaged about 1,300 feet of timber per car. After the trees had been harvested, the men would load the rails, ties, and anchor spikes on the cars for transport to the next cutting area where the rail system would be reinstalled.

Even the several structures needed for each camp depended on the Shay. While most camp buildings were constructed of logs, the Shay made it more efficient to build structures with processed lumber at the mill. The lumber would be sawed to meet certain specifications and along with the hardware would be transported to the campsite where it would be assembled. Later it would be taken down and transported by the Shay to the next cutting area where it would be re-installed.

While Shay's invention was intended for his own use, it soon attracted the attention of local lumbermen and beyond. Cadillac timber and manufacturing companies, including Cobbs and Mitchell, Cummer and Diggins, and the Mitchell Brothers purchased at least 24 Shays.

After William Crippen's machine shop and the Michigan Iron Works of Cadillac made a few of the locomotives, Shay moved his manufacturing operation to the Lima (Ohio) Machine Works. The move launched the Lima facility into becoming one of the nation's largest locomotive manufacturers. Many Shays were shipped throughout the US and abroad where they would be used by mining and tourist sites, as well as timber harvests.

About 2,770 Shay locomotives were manufactured. The last Shay left the factory assembly line in Lima in 1945.

Several Shay locomotives are in museum displays throughout the US including in the states of Maryland, California, Texas, Tennessee, Michigan, Ohio, and Florida.

Following his successful timber harvest and processing operation in Haring Township, Shay moved to Harbor Springs where he opened another logging business. He continued his inventiveness that included the construction of a 40 foot long steel steamboat. He died in 1916 at age 77 and is buried in Harbor Springs.

CAMPS, JACKS, AND HORSES

The Cook Staff at Mitchell Camp No. 33

The men who cut down the trees and moved them to the mills faced constant danger and difficult working conditions. Because snow and ice made log hauling in the forest much easier, most of the tree harvesting took place from early December to late March. At harvest areas near railways, cutting went on year around as the logs could be "skidded" by horse-drawn Big Wheels. Chains placed under the logs would be used to raise the front of the logs between the two nine-foot diameter wheels where they could be dragged short distances by horses.

A typical logging camp would have a manager, a few highly experienced lumberjacks and from 15 to 75 workers including jacks, cooks, a nurse, horse attendants and a blacksmith. Managers were continually challenged to maintain production efficiency while keeping camp

TIMBER TOWN TALES

morale high. A Wexford County camp might consist of a large building that served as a bunkhouse and dining hall, a horse barn with a repair shop, and a cook's house for food storage and preparation. Usually the structures would be reassembled from the processed lumber of an earlier camp.

Soon after the timber manager defined a cutting area, an experienced logger would survey the topography and mark the trees to be cut. The large eastern white pines reached heights of 150 feet with a three- to five-foot trunk diameter measured at the level of a man's chest. With an axe he would cut a wedge to provide the lumberjacks with the precise direction each tree must fall. The cutting sequence and the direction of the fall were crucial. Adequate space was planned for the horses with their cumbersome sleds to be placed where the heavy logs could be loaded and transported to a rail or waterway. Jacks would dig sled tracks one foot deep and one foot wide to be filled with water and left to freeze overnight, making it easier for the horses to pull their loads.

The company treated their jacks very well. They were well paid, well fed and openly appreciated by management. When injured on the job, the company paid their recovery costs. After their evening meal, the jacks would sharpen and oil their saws, axes, chains and other tools. A camp store sold tobacco, sweets and stationery. In their quarters, some strummed their musical instruments while others practiced their dance floor steps with each other. Games and storytelling provided a less active entertainment.

Today, some criticize early lumber barons for their clear-cutting practices. While it would be nice to have a few more groves of white pines such as the Hartwick Pines State Park near Grayling, the mindsets of that period seemed to assume an endless supply of trees. The late 19th century was a time of rapidly increasing numbers of immigrants caused by a multitude of worldwide conditions. Michigan, the nation's leading lumber producer at that time, played a major role in providing the construction, flooring and other manufactured wood products needed for building and furnishing structures to accommodate the new populations.

Further, after the harvesting reached its peak during the early 20th century, new forests emerged. Numerous species of trees appeared. Those cut over fields soon began yielding berries and other edibles that fed a much greater variety and vastly increased number of animals and birds.

It might be argued that 19th century timber harvesting made possible the many nature-related recreational experiences we enjoy today.

THE ICEMEN CAME

The Huckleberry and Watson Ice and Coal Company workers are shown in front of their ice hoist at their large ice storage facility on West Chapin Street.

Besides very big trees, the Clam Lake area boasted another economic bonanza; two large lakes and cold winters! By the winter 1872-73, several crude structures appeared along the shores of both lakes where local entrepreneurs cut, stored, and sold blocks of ice of various sizes to the villagers and shopkeepers. An industry was born!

Following are some observations about that industry's considerable economic influence on the Village of Clam Lake (City of Cadillac in 1877.)

William Cassler built Clam Lake's first icehouse on the water's edge at the foot of Chapin Street. He sold his business to Mr. Huckleberry, who later brought on Mr.

Watson as his partner. Ice was delivered to Cadillac homes through the 1930s on horse drawn enclosed carts. Huckleberry and Watson's large icehouse was razed in May 1951.

As early as March 1874, harvesting ice had become an important exporting business. Thirty carloads of the hundreds filled with the block ice were shipped to Cincinnati that month. For the ensuing month it was estimated that it would take a 15-car train, departing daily for five months, to transport all of the ice stored in Clam Lake ice houses. These data are particularly impressive given that the ice cutting and transporting to railways depended entirely on manpower and horsepower until the late 1870's when steam-powered cutting tools appeared. Motor-powered ice harvesting machines did not arrive until about 1912.

Warm Decembers in southern Michigan and other states generated an accelerated harvest preparation plan that would include substantial expansions of work crews and storage houses. The winter of 1877 – 1878 was unusually warm and the demand for ice rose markedly. A Kentucky man made the long trip to Cadillac to plead for 200 carloads to be sent to his state immediately. The two large icehouses would be left empty before the season ended. Risks taken to meet customer demands resulted in horses breaking through the ice, although no horse fatalities were reported. Crews worked around the clock cutting and either floating or carting the blocks of ice to the icehouses. The demand led to the formation of several new harvesting companies.

Another harvest season of note occurred during the winter of 1889-1890. Companies from Adrian in southern Michigan and other states set up ice harvesting facilities on area lakes. The Toledo Coal and Ice Company erected storage buildings on Big Clam Lake (Lake Mitchell) where they would store 100,000 tons of ice and send out about 100 cars of ice a day. At one point, area storage facilities held 174,500 tons of cut ice harvested from the two Cadillac lakes, Fife, Round, Long, Crooked, and Muskrat

(Missaukee) lakes. This large volume required 600 to 800 men from the Cadillac and Lake City areas to harvest the ice, transport it to local storage facilities, and load the blocks for shipment to southern Michigan and out of state buyers during the summer months.

Because most of the labor was seasonal, the well-paid workers rented rooms, visited entertainment venues, and dined in local restaurants thereby benefitting immeasurably the local economy.

The lumber industry in Cadillac at that time generated many times the volume of business activity produced by the ice harvesters. Both industries required crews to be at their work sites primarily during the winter months. It's no wonder that the two rail systems, the Grand Rapids and Indiana and the Toledo, Ann Arbor, and Northern Michigan, totaled 15 to 20 departures each day hauling Cadillac area products to their southern markets.

MADE IN CADILLAC

Shown are employees in front of a portion of the Cadillac Handle Company which was located near Wright Street, at the present location of a plant owned by Mitchell Corporation. Cadillac Handle Company produced 20,000 feet of lumber and about 125,000 broom handles each day. The company was owned by the Mitchell & Cobbs Lumber Interests and was under the direction of A. W. Newark. The handle plant closed in 1920 when its timber became exausted.

The Cadillac Handle Factory staff, c.1905. Included are Harry Zelma, August Anderson, Oscar Peterson, Oliver Sterling, John Gilbert, and Peter Benson.

Soon after the Village of Clam Lake was founded in 1871, white pine trees were harvested and lakeside mills were built to convert the timbers into construction lumber. Within weeks, the large companies as well as smaller independent entrepreneurs launched a variety of "spin-off" initiatives that resulted in a wide variety of wood, chemical, agricultural and metal products for export.

Cobbs and Mitchell, Inc. established a Chemical plant on Little Clam Lake, at the foot of current Pearl Street, where they made wood alcohol, acetate of lime and charcoal. In 1877, the company cut one million feet of logs into 6-inch x 26-inch x 29-feet timbers for the reconstruction of the Welland Canal, at St. Catharines, Ontario. Later they opened the 600-feet by 200-feet Electric Flooring mill on the northwest corner of South and South Mitchell streets.

The gigantic Cummer-Diggins operation was located on the northeast shore of Lake Cadillac. Along with construction lumber and flooring, the company manufactured many innovative products that served buyers worldwide. They pioneered the design of hinged folding crates that found customers as far away as South Africa. The famous "Humpty-Dumpty" egg transport crates proved to be a popular item. Wooden bust forms were "well received" by Marshall Field's Department Store in Chicago. Other products included 100,000 wooden bleacher seats for Detroit, stepladders, breadboards, cabinets, bureaus, picture frames, doors, tables and various chemical products.

The Cadillac Handle Company, located in the recent fire-destroyed Mitchell-Bentley building on Wright Street, made 125,000 broom handles a day. The Cadillac Turpentine Company extracted wood fibers from stumps of harvested pine trees to make and sell turpentine to domestic and overseas markets. A few small shops made medicines and livestock food from charcoal. In December 1890, John Vosberg shipped about 10,000 Christmas trees to the "big city" in one day. Cadillac Veneer and Basket produced drawer bottoms, cheese hoops, picture backs and fruit boxes. The Sash and Door Company shipped large quantities of screen doors to points south.

Farmer Bergland shipped wool to Boston and E. Minges of Colfax Township sent maple sugar to Sacramento. Cornwall made a grain-hulling machine for a company in Omaha. McAdie Iron Works manufactured two six-ton steam engines for the Oval Dish Factory in Traverse City. In 1886, the Hixon mill made and sold 40,000 metal barrel straps a day. A large steaming vat invented by locals Moody and Haines of the Cadillac Boiler

Works, was shipped to Pratt in Buffalo. During 1894, three-fourths of a ton of potash to make munitions and soap was shipped to New York each week and carloads of "wasted" wood was frequently sent to Chicago for fireplaces. The Michigan Iron Works, manufacturers of the first Shay locomotives, made logging engines for companies throughout Michigan. They also made a cannon!

Most of the products mentioned above were first sent to markets before 1900. In 1906, the Cadillac State Bank summarized a state factory inspector's "conservative" report on Cadillac's industrial activity. In part, it read:

"Cadillac's thirty factories employed 1,660 hands (distributed among) six lumber mills, three planing mills, two flooring plants, a 125-ton charcoal iron plant, two chemical and charcoal plants, a last block factory (shoe molds,) a veneer and basket works, a handle factory, a crate factory, iron works and machine shop, cooperage (wooden barrels) stock mill, collar factory, six cigar factories, brickyard, two grist mills, table factory, cabinet works, and at least twenty smaller institutions employing from half a dozen to twenty-five hands.

"Several of Cadillac's industries are the largest of their kind in the world. Cadillac maple flooring has made a reputation from the dining room of the White House to re-built Frisco and here is located the largest flooring plant in the world."

The tiny village built on rolling hills overlooking two pleasant lakes soon became an industrial powerhouse that captured a nation's attention.

TIMBER TOWN TALES

TIMBERS TO TATERS

Amos Nixon built this barn in Cherry Grove Township, ca.1903. The same family has owned the farm for several generations.

Our area's first settlers rarely considered raising food crops in the Clam Lake region. White pine trees dominated the lakes area making the land undesirable for agriculture purposes.

Acreage with hardwood stands a few miles away from Clam Lake were quite satisfactory for a variety of crops after trees were removed, but the task of preparing the soil for crops was costly.

The Homestead Act of 1862 provided for the distribution of 160-acre plots of land to residents who would receive deeds to the property if they resided on the piece for five years and grew sustainable crops.

Civil War veterans could reduce the five-year requirement by their time served in the military. Much of Wexford County was claimed under the act and the first generation settlers were able to make a living by leasing or harvesting trees for the mills. When they were unable to sustain a livelihood off the acreage, the land would be forfeited back to the U.S. government. Additional tracts of land owned by the harvesting companies were abandoned after the tree harvest. Much of that land made up the Manistee National Forest, established in 1938, and would become the Huron-Manistee National Forest in 1945.

Although crop soil in the immediate area was not good, Cadillac became an important processing and distribution center for agricultural products.

Beginning in the late 19th century, nearby Missaukee and Osceola counties and parts of Wexford County had good success harvesting wheat, hay, corn, rutabagas, oats, carrots, beets and other varieties of vegetable. Livestock and dairy products also became exportable commodities.

The first annual fair of the Wexford County Agricultural, Industrial, and Pomological (fruit cultivation) Society was held in Cadillac in October 1883. There were no cash awards for the best farm products. Winners were issued "diplomas" for prize horses, cattle, sheep, swine, poultry, grain, flour, meal, fruit, butter, cheese, bread, pickles, preserves, fancy work and more. Also recognized were the best lumber wagon, double buggy, single buggy and plow.

The timber barons and sheepherders provided evidence of a community working together. During fall 1891, Charley Crosby and his 300 sheep occupied the vacated Cummer camp in Haring Township. In 1893, the Mitchell Brothers, developers of the large Jennings timber-processing center, provided winter quarters for 640 sheep on their ranch northeast of Cadillac.

Potatoes were the only significant exportable

product of Wexford County, although many other crops of good quality were grown on small plots for local consumption. The volatility of the markets faced by farmers today was experienced by earlier generations as well. In June of 1913, the price of potatoes fell to 7 cents a bushel. In September of that year they were selling for 70 cents a bushel. That same year, Wexford County potatoes dominated awards among the state's potato farmers and in 1918, Cadillac was chosen as headquarters for the Michigan Potato Growers Exchange.

By 1910, much land had been cleared of stumps and Wexford County became more significant as an agricultural center. Early farmers found rich topsoil, but later discovered that it was very thin. In 1914, a serious move was made to make Cadillac an apple-growing center. Alfalfa and sweet clover made a big impact on markets in 1926. In August 1927 the county farm population was 5,097 on 1,328 farms. A muskrat ranch was established at Wheeler Creek in Cherry Grove Township and in the 1930s, Wexford County revealed a trend toward dairy cattle.

In 1928 the Michigan State College of Agriculture (MSU) bought 480 acres near Lake City for a potato experimental farm.

TIMBER TOWN TALES

RURAL SCHOOLS OF WEXFORD COUNTY

1- Myrtle Fires
2- David Carlson
3- Sylvia Fires
4
5. Elsie Carlson
6. Roy Drill
7- Glen Stark
8 Marjorie Andrews
9 Grace Austin
10 Sylvan Fires
11 Theo. Schabr
12 Otis Fires
13 Vern Andrews
14 May Brown
15 Carl Carlson
16 Grace Mort
17 Frank Chase
18 Alfred

Students enrolled at the Conant School near Hoxeyville, South Branch Township, June 1912.

"Cultivate a sweet, mellow, firm voice. A loud harsh voice irritates pupils. A soft answer turneth away wrath ... be clean ... dress neatly. No gaudy clothes, nor old party dresses." These are among a long list of "Suggestions to Teachers" that appeared in the Wexford County Schools report of 1912-13. It was also suggested that the teachers "keep the school yard clean ... sweep and dust the school room every day… keep the outhouses clean and sanitary ... conduct short, snappy early morning exercises." Not coincidently, perhaps, the American Federation of Teachers was founded in 1916.

TIMBER TOWN TALES

The Cornell School, established in 1865, was Wexford County's first school. The log school, built by volunteers, was located at the intersection of Four and Eleven Mile roads in Wexford Township, close to the Grand Traverse County line. The first teacher, Miss Zylphia Harper, collected her pay from the parents of attending children.

More than 80 rural schools were opened in Wexford County between 1865 and 1905. There were several rural schools in each of the county's 16 townships. To make it practical for students to walk to their classes, schools were built no more than two miles from each other. Many were constructed around the lumber camps and as the tree harvests were completed, the schools would often move with the camps to the next cutting area. Others were built along sidings of the Grand Rapids and Indiana and the Toledo, Ann Arbor, and Northern Michigan railways. Some of the schools and their replacement structures continued instruction well into the 1960s. A few of the buildings are occupied today as homes, churches, and community centers.

A teacher would usually board with a student's family as part of her compensation. Enrollments in the one-room elementary schools would range from sometimes less than a dozen and up to 30 or more pupils. Teachers were responsible for keeping the schoolroom clean, the fires burning and the kerosene lanterns lit. They often called on their students to assist with some of the maintenance. Students in the upper grades would assist the younger ones with their lessons.

A "Teacher's Summary Report," completed by an Antioch Township teacher in 1908 provides a glimpse into the characteristics of rural schools of that era. There were seven boys and 14 girls registered in Miss Maud's school. The class achieved an average daily attendance record of 16 students. Only six students were tardy and two were neither tardy nor absent. The value of the school "apparatus" was estimated at $1,000. There were 100 volumes in the school library and 50 trees on the school grounds. The whole number of days taught was 100 and the teacher was compensated at $42 per month. The average tuition cost per student each month was one dollar.

Much of the information for this story was taken from a 48-page booklet, "Rural Schools of Wexford County," published by the Wexford County Historical Society in 1981. Society members Edward Babcock and James Comp compiled that important work. Township maps briefly describe and provide the locations of the schools. Included are photographs of some of the schools. A full county map also displays the early Indian trails from Cadillac northward to the Grand Traverse County line.

Babcock (my Cadillac High School chemistry and physics teacher) wrote in his Forward: "By the 1930s, legislators and educators decided that centralization and consolidation were essential. Proponents of the idea didn't claim that consolidation ensured better education. Instead they felt that it would offer a greater range of studies at lower cost. Teachers could be paid better salaries and education throughout the country would be equalized."

Rural schools provided at least adequate learning environments and generally highly favorable social settings for the children. Certain features of those American institutions applied to today's classrooms might prove to be rather beneficial.

CADILLAC HIGH SCHOOL

School spirit at Cadillac High School during the late 19th Century.

It was mid-June 1872, a month before his new village was platted, that Clam Lake's founder George A. Mitchell, set aside the square block now occupied by Kirtland Terrace as a permanent site for the school. That decision sent a profound message: The education of Clam Lake's children would be a high priority.

The site selected was at "an elevation commanding a most beautiful view of the town." More importantly, it was within a two-minute walk to the village center and the homes of most of the community's leading citizens.

By early 1873, there were 35 enrollees in the Clam Lake Public School and in 1877 a high school unit was added, graduating its first class in 1883. The graduation ceremony was held before a large crowd at the Opera House on Beech Street.

On March 8, 1884, arson was suspected in a fire that destroyed the two-story wood-constructed building along with all furnishings and books. A comparable replacement structure also burned in 1890.

A magnificent brick structure was then erected and remained on the site until it was razed for the Kirtland Terrace apartment building. When the new school was opened in 1891, J. W. Cobbs, W. W. Cummer and W. W. Mitchell gifted a large clock, seven feet in diameter with dials facing all four directions. A hammer was made to strike the 1,500-pound bell every 30 minutes with the appropriate number strikes indicating the on-the-hour times. The large weights that propelled the bell would rise and fall a distance of 27 feet.

In 1894, Cadillac High School graduates became eligible for admission to the University of Michigan without examination after an onsite accreditation visit report by a UM faculty member. Only eight of the 70 accredited Michigan high schools at that time were located in northern Michigan (defined here as north of highway M-55.) It is noteworthy that those seven other schools, Alpena, Manistee, Traverse City, Houghton, Hancock, Ishpeming and Marquette, are all located on a Great Lakes shore and were first settled at least 15 years before Clam Lake was platted. (Note: To find this information, I contacted a 1974 Cadillac High School graduate, Nancy Bartlett, who is the Acting Associate Director of the highly respected Bentley

TIMBER TOWN TALES

Historical Library at the University of Michigan. Her colleague, archivist Brian Williams, conducted the research for us.)

A personal experience has helped convince me of our school's traditional excellence. Soon after I arrived at my new administrative position at the University of Michigan in 1964, the financial aid director greeted me with heartwarming story.

Ivan Parker remembered well a year in the early 1950s when five or six Cadillac High School graduates were among the 100 University's School of Medicine admissions. He told me that because of the medical school's national reputation, it was rare to see more than two admissions offers to students from one secondary school.

The Vikings won the first Michigan interscholastic basketball tournament, held in East Lansing in 1919. The football team won the state championship in 1950 and many of those athletes led Cadillac to a state track and field title the following spring. Alpine state skiing championships have been won.

In her interesting book, "100 Seasons of Cadillac High School Football," Sue Starkweather compiled statistics of Viking football squads from 1896 through 1993. Cadillac won 57 percent of the 757 games played, lost 37 percent, and tied 6 percent. Of our major rivals, those played five or more times during that period, the Vikings had a winning percentage versus 21 of those 25 teams. Strong academics and well-conducted sports programs go very well together.

In "The Tempest" Shakespeare penned, "Whereof what's past is prologue, what to come, in yours and my discharge." George Mitchell's school site decision of 142 years ago has been well "discharged." We live in a community that continues to embrace his well-placed educational priorities.

THE MICHIGAN WILDCAT

The John Wolgast family. Adolph ("Ad"), the oldest of the Wolgast children, is seated between his parents.

Adolph "Ad" Wolgast, a Cadillac professional boxer, became the lightweight boxing champion of the world after he defeated Oscar "Battling" Nelson on February 22, 1910 in Point Richmond, California. Ring Magazine ranked that 40-round fight, attended by a crowd of 18,000, as 19th of the "100 Greatest Fights of All Time."

The Wolgast family lived on their Whaley Road farm. The father, John Wolgast, is listed in the 1900 Cadillac City Directory as a cigar-maker. "Ad," born Jan. 8, 1888, was the oldest of seven children. His brothers, Al and Johnny, were also boxers. Johnny, a middleweight, is listed in the

TIMBER TOWN TALES

Pennsylvania Sports Hall of Fame.

Ad Wolgast's professional career was launched in June 1906 at age 18. By the end of the year he had fought and won 13 times, mostly by knockouts. Ten of those contests were held in Grand Rapids, two in Petoskey, and one in Lansing. The next two years he fought in Milwaukee and in February 1909 he moved to California. During his first two and one-half years as a professional, he fought 66 fights losing only once. While he preferred the moniker, "The Cadillac Kid," he became widely known as "The Michigan Wildcat."

According to Tracy Callis an International Research Boxing Organization historian, "Wolgast was a scrappy, durable, determined brawler deluxe with great stamina and a stiff punch."

After defeating "Battling" Nelson, he won 24 fights without a loss as champion, five of which were defending his title. On Nov. 28, 1912 Willie Ritchie defeated him on a foul call, only his second official loss in more than 80 contests. ("Official" organizations and the newspapers employed different won / loss definitions.) The following six years that included more than 50 fights, he attained an unimpressive record, while enduring broken arms and ribs, damage to his eyes, ears, nose and serious trauma to his brain.

He suffered a nervous breakdown in 1918 and was committed to a sanitarium. He was later given over to the care of a boxing promoter who allowed him to continue living his dream. For seven years, Wolgast trained vigorously every day believing he would again compete for the title. Most likely due to his good looks and fame, he landed roles and consultations in two movies, "Some Punches and Judy" (1923) and "The Prince of Broadway," (1926.)

In April 1923, Wolgast's mother received a telegram that her son had died in California. As plans were made to return his body to Michigan, it was discovered that the dead man was Ed Wolgast of Peoria.

After a violent episode in California, he was

considered insane, the result of too many "blows to the head." Ad's health continued to decline and in 1927, he was committed to the Stockton State Hospital in California where he spent the remaining years of his life. At age 61, Wolgast was left permanently disabled when severely beaten by two guards eager to "test the toughness" of the legendary boxer.

"The Michigan Wildcat" died on April 14, 1955 at age 67 in California. Charley Rose, a leading boxing rater, ranked Wolgast the 9th All-Time best lightweight boxer in the world. According to the Cyber Boxing Zone, Wolgast was elected to the Ring Hall of Fame in 1958 and the International Boxing Hall of Fame in 2000.

Much has been written both locally and nationally about the 5-feet, 4-inch, 120-pound pugilist. He was very proud of his home community. When introduced as a Milwaukee or California resident, he quickly corrected the announcer with, "I am from Cadillac, Michigan."

During his world championship reign, he returned to Michigan to marry Mildred Ensign of Cadillac on Feb. 18, 1911.

THE LADIES WANTED A LIBRARY

The Cadillac Public Library was considered one of the most expensive and elaborate of the 53 Carnegie libraries built in Michigan.

Most early-recorded history is about the achievements of men. Gender-specific home and work responsibilities during the 19th and early 20th centuries differed considerably from those of today.

There were, however, a number of Cadillac women who were concerned about the level of literacy in their community and they did something about it.

The Clam Lake Ladies Library Association was formed in June 1876 with responsibility for "The maintenance, enlargement, and use of a library of such character as will conduce to advancement of its members socially, mentally, and morally."

This small group, also known as the Ladies Penelopean Society, began collecting books and raising funds from local citizens. They paid annual dues, sponsored entertainment programs, and held rummage sales, which brought several hundred dollars into their meager treasury.

The library was first located in the old Holbrook and May Hall and later in the Congregational Church annex.

The need for a permanent structure was first addressed in 1901 when the board submitted a request to the Andrew Carnegie Foundation. To meet the terms of the $15,000 Carnegie gift, the board was required to 1) demonstrate the need for a public library, 2) provide a building site, 3) commit to an annual operational support of at least 10 percent of the construction cost, and, 4) provide free service for all.

The site was a gift from Jacob Cummer. William Mitchell, Delos Diggins, Jacob Cummer and Wellington Cummer donated grant-matching funds.

The Cadillac Public Library with 3,000 volumes on its shelves, opened in its new Beech Street building on September 7, 1906. With its classical revival style architecture it has been recognized as one of the most expensive and elaborate of the 53 Carnegie libraries built in Michigan.

W. F. Sanborn was appointed as the first librarian and janitor at $60 a month, a position he held until his death in 1926. In 1912 a doctor acquired a box to disinfect books returned from patrons who may have carried contagious diseases.

Mary C. Ramsey replaced Sanborn as head librarian and held the position for the next 25 years.

The Wexford County library was created in Cadillac in January 1935 and by February 1939 was serving 40 rural schools. The Works Progress Administration (WPA,) a U.S. Great Depression relief organization contributed 477 books. Another 1,500 were on loan from the state library.

Gladys Cardinal was the lead librarian and the WPA provided assistants. When branch libraries were established in Mesick, Boon and Harrietta, Cardinal shuttled the books in her car.

TIMBER TOWN TALES

In 1936 an old school bus was purchased and remodeled into a bookmobile. It was the first of its kind in northern Michigan and one of only two in the state.

That service was discontinued during World War II, but re-started in 1946 when Alice Stafford became the bookmobile librarian. The Wexford County Library purchased a new shelved bookmobile in 1951 and in June 1953 a garage to store the vehicle was built next to the library. (Stafford provided me the opportunity to drive the bookmobile route one summer. That memorable experience consisted of loading the vehicle with books, a 16mm movie and projector, and visit schools and township centers to the delight of hundreds of rural bookmobile visitors.)

The city and county libraries with their 14,000 and 12,000 books, respectively, merged in 1953 to become the Cadillac and Wexford County Public Library, the first such merger in Michigan.

In 1962, the library was selected as headquarters library to service the 10 counties comprising the Mid-Michigan League Area (37 libraries in Missaukee, Wexford, Manistee, Roscommon, Mecosta, Osceola, Lake, Mason, Oceana and Newaygo counties.)

Because of deteriorating conditions and a lack of space the need for a new building arose. In May 1968 voters approved a plan to construct a new library on Lake Street. Federal funds provided two-thirds of the $600,000 construction costs. Local funds ($200,000) and donations ($12,000) provided the necessary additional funding.

After the replacement library was completed in 1969, the Cadillac Police Department occupied the Carnegie building temporarily. When the Police Department was relocated in 1977, the structure was considered for demolition to provide space for a parking structure. Fortunately, the Wexford County Historical Society intervened and saved the community treasure as a county museum.

BOYS BEHAVING BADLY

Confiscated "moonshine" equipment is displayed near the Wexford County jail. Sheriff Charles Nixon stands at the right, c. 1920s.

It has been reported that the growth of Clam Lake during the summer of 1872 was unprecedented in the history of Michigan. By May of 1873, less than a year after Clam Lake was platted, the number of village residents had reached 1,000. This population explosion had a substantial impact on a village that lacked a political structure, organized management, fire and crime fighting institutions, and other community services.

The promise of high paying jobs for the skilled and unskilled alike attracted mostly young men and teenagers, including large numbers of recently landed immigrants from northern Europe and Canada. A small, but rapidly growing number of young women arrived to wait tables and entertain the young men.

Well-paid, hard-working men and boys would sometimes misbehave. Most of the lawlessness was fueled by an overindulgence of alcohol and consisted mostly of barroom brawls and drunken behaviors in the village's 15 or more drinking establishments. George Mitchell and his colleagues needed to find ways to set up a legal system and build a jailhouse to maintain the peace.

Most Clam Lake crimes would be considered misdemeanors today. A mid-night "rampage" in Mr. Pope's bar resulted in dozens of smashed glasses. A 10-year-old boy was placed in jail overnight for stealing a wallet. A blacksmith and a lumberjack had a fight won by the blacksmith. A watch charm was clipped from a man's chain during baptism. A stranger in town who stole a wallet in Mrs. Graham's restaurant was grabbed by her and held until the police arrived. Men who stole two ducks and 36 chickens were captured and sent to prison. A man in a wig and a dress was jailed because he infringed on women's sole right to wear false hair. A man was nearly lynched by a mob at Idlewild Park for injuring a woman who would not dance with him. Another man was fined five dollars for putting his aged mother-in-law out of the house. A man was found guilty for serving beer to guests in his own home. (That man had his conviction reversed by the State Supreme Court.) Fights caused snow to be red with blood caused by "dumb or inhuman brutes."

After the Ohio House Hotel was called the "most notorious place in town," the keeper pulled up stakes and left the village, which according to the newspaper "is good riddance." A house of "ill-repute" on GR & I RR property was encircled by a rope and pulled to its destruction by a locomotive. Citizens urged that houses of "ill-fame" on West Mason Street be moved out of town. Miss Minnie Brown "strayed up here from Big Rapids or some other bad town." Minnie "was not a good girl so the sheriff took her to the Detroit House of Corrections."

In 1877, the Detroit Post described Clam Lake as "the wickedest place in the mid-west" and the Cleveland News added that the village was a "haven of harlots and saloon-keepers." Clam Lake's mayor, known as an "honest, sensible man" made a serious proposal to legalize prostitution. He was labeled a "sybarite" (hedonist) and his community a "sink of iniquity." A few years later the Detroit Free Press labeled Cadillac "the smartest and most promising city in northern Michigan."

Before a jail was constructed in Clam Lake, law violators would be retained in GR & I RR boxcars or sent to Reed City and Big Rapids jails. During the early years, jail breaks included prying off roof boards, cutting through brick, tearing up the cell floor and digging their way out, and receiving tools handed between bars from friends on the outside.

An 1891 ordinance prohibited nude bathing in city waters between 5 a.m. and 8 p.m. That ordinance was repealed in June 1967. (Gee! Was nude bathing allowed at night in Lake Cadillac when I was a teen-ager?")

TIMBER TOWN TALES

THEY OUGHTA MAKE A MOVIE

A view of a children's event from the Lyric Theatre Stage, c. 1930's or early 1940's.

While researching stories for the Cadillac News, I often wonder why someone hasn't captured the many stimulating elements of our unique early history and produced a Hollywood "blockbuster."

The late 19th Century was the time-period of the "westerns" where the good guys wore white hats and the bad guys were either rich or robbed the rich. Cows, horses, guns, barrooms and a sheriff dominated the story lines many, many times. Let's examine some possible story settings about our late 19th century history.

A very rich good guy, George Mitchell, (Tom

TIMBER TOWN TALES

Hanks?) founded a village (Clam Lake?) and welcomed hordes of young men by promising them high salaries to harvest giant trees and process the timber in the local mills.

Life in the camps and forests was characterized by danger, maybe a bit of intrigue, and interesting personal relationships among good, hard-working men. Our village founder recruited other good rich guys who were experienced industrialists and who soon became both his friends and his corporate rivals in the small, picturesque community.

So, who are the bad guys? My earlier story on "Boys Behaving Badly" briefly described the "activities" of an interesting cast of characters. Strong virile men with money attracted women to comfort and entertain them, often for a price.

Several trains arrived daily bringing charlatans and snake-oil salesmen oftentimes of devious character, while the little village operated without a law enforcement structure in place.

One particular true story from a late 19th century Cadillac newspaper illustrates that truth frequently trumps fiction.

On an April 1890 morning the Hotel Jackson room ledger included the name of women rights activist, Belva Lockwood, (Susan Sarandon?) an ex-presidential candidate twice and the first woman to argue a case before the U.S. Supreme Court.

The newspaper reported that joining the feisty Lockwood at the hotel dining table that evening were six preachers of the Presbytery who were in session in Cadillac for the week, four gamblers that "belonged to the too numerous gang that infest Cadillac," and a murderer and a horse-thief who were in transit with two police officers to Benzonia for their trial.

A script for the dinnertime conversation could be rather entertaining.

A few real-life characters might be portrayed. A scrappy young professional boxer, Ad Wolgast, (small, tough guy?) became a lightweight champion of the world. The Michigan Wildcat lived a colorful albeit tragic life.

Dr. John Leeson (George Clooney?) created and distributed throughout the country an elixir, Tiger Oil that was advertised to cure nearly all ills suffered by man or beast. A story of his varied and highly productive life would be displayed with a comedic slant.

Delos Diggins (Richard Gere?) died a short time before the opening of the hospital (sorry Richard) he had built for his village. Later, his grieving wife, Esther, (Meryl Streep?) provided funds for construction that more than doubled the size of the high school.

Ephraim Shay's (Jeff Daniels?) powerful little locomotive, designed and first manufactured in Cadillac, revolutionized not only timber harvesting, but also mining throughout the world.

Present day Cadillac is also well positioned for the camera work with buildings such as the Cobbs and Mitchell office building, County Court House, old City Hall, Museum, and the homes of Delos Cobbs, George A. Mitchell, William W. Mitchell, and several Historic District homes. Toss in the museum and the Ann Arbor Railroad Depot, Maple Hill Cemetery, Kenwood Park, the canal, and the many hills, forests, and waters of our area and we can begin writing script and recruiting a cast.

SABOTEURS AND TOASTERS

Keep cool, save time, save steps and cook better this summer with a

CADILLAC
Combination Electric Stove and Toaster

It will cook eggs on the grid above the coils and toast in the drawer below at the same time, at your breakfast table. Simply attach to any light socket and turn the button. You can regulate the heat as desired and keep things warm at the table. Finished in nickel and black enamel and sent prepaid on receipt of $7.50.

Cadillac Electric Mfg. Co., 216 Mitchell St. Cadillac, Mich.

This ad was created c.1910

Thanks to our area's remarkable history, my retired life has

TIMBER TOWN TALES

been enriched immeasurably by my varied museum volunteer projects.

When we launched our Website a few years ago through the Cadillac News web service, CNDigital Solution, I somewhat thoughtlessly agreed to handle viewers questions submitted to our website. Since then, I have responded to hundreds of inquiries from all over the U.S. and many foreign countries. Because the site is "name & place searchable," many inquiries are from Sweden and other northern European countries seeking long-lost relatives.

Most foreign inquiries, however, come from Ireland. The Irish, too, have a Wexford County Museum and I rather enjoy responding to those who mistakenly find us as they seek information from our namesake county museum in Ireland.

A few years ago, an Ann Arbor researcher emailed me about a German saboteur who set fires and destroyed chemical factories in several Michigan cities during World War I. He suspected that Cadillac was one of his targets. Having read and indexed the two celebratory issues of the Cadillac Evening News that included an historical chronology of thousands of news items dating from 1871, I responded that it was unlikely such an event took place in Cadillac. I added that if I had the approximate date of the event, I would "see what I could find." Later, when I accessed our Cadillac Evening News index, I found the following 1916 chronology entry:

May 18 — "The Cadillac Chemical Co. group of buildings was destroyed by fire starting about noon. The company was making chemicals for war purposes and its product was in the greatest demand in the concern's history at high prices. The loss is estimated at $50,000. Next day Charles T. Mitchell, president, said the plant would be rebuilt as soon as possible."

My researcher friend was delighted with our find that validated his supposition. No mention of the fire was included in a feature story about the chemical plant. The facility was located in the Cobbs and Mitchell complex about where a Pearl Street extension would end at Lake Cadillac on Holly Road. Their products included wood alcohol and acetate of lime, both used in the manufacture of explosives. They also made pig iron from the charcoal residue. According to the inquirer, the company's products were shipped to England and France for their military uses against the Germans prior to America's entry into the war in 1917.

Another interesting inquiry concerned toasters.

"Did you know that your community is historically significant as a maker of toasters?" was the question. It was submitted by the editor of the Saturday Evening Toast (no joke!) who claimed that a small firm, the Cadillac Electric Manufacturing Company, was the second U.S. manufacturer of toasters. General Electric made the first toasters.

The small company, organized in Reed City, moved to 216 South Mitchell Street in Cadillac where it was incorporated on December 29, 1910. The short chronology entry included, "... they planned to manufacture a light electric stove."

The toaster, depicted here, was a combination stove and toaster that was engineered to have the entire breakfast prepared for eating at the same time. One ad displays a man reading his morning paper and drinking coffee while his breakfast was being prepared beside him. Google "Cadillac Toaster" and enjoy several views of a product created and manufactured in Cadillac and still displayed at toaster-collectors conventions around the U.S. Unfortunately, we do not have this important historical product to display and we would be most appreciative if one were to be gifted to the Society.

Our very active website with its 150 hits a day continues to yield a number of historical events that might never have otherwise been revealed.

TIMBER TOWN TALES

BALLOTS AND ORDINANCES

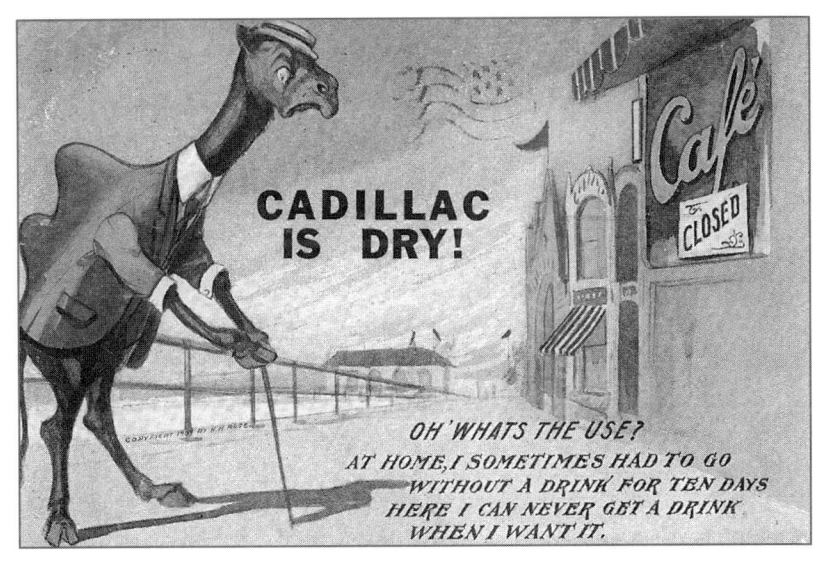

CADILLAC IS DRY!

OH WHAT'S THE USE?
AT HOME, I SOMETIMES HAD TO GO
WITHOUT A DRINK FOR TEN DAYS
HERE I CAN NEVER GET A DRINK
WHEN I WANT IT.

The people have spoken!

Before 1900, there were few political issues that were settled by popular votes.

The people elected commissioners, supervisors, trustees, councils and other ruling bodies to make decisions for the communities they were elected to serve.

The final location of the Wexford County seat was among those early Wexford County issues that required popular votes.

During October 1881, after 17 resolutions, the county supervisors finally selected Manton as the county seat, where it had been moved from Sherman. That site was strongly supported by the northern and western township and village supervisors for its proximity advantage for their citizens.

When the site-decision was presented for the

required countywide popular vote Cadillac, with its strong population advantage, won the seat in the April 1882 election by a 1,363 to 636 vote. (*A lengthy essay penned by Judge William R. Peterson on the county seat location controversy is featured in the 1971 Cadillac Evening News Centennial issue beginning on page A-2. Go to www.wexfordcountyhistory.org Home Page and click on Wexford County History. Under Primary Sources find Cadillac Evening News and follow instructions for the digitized version.*)

During the early years of the new century, Wexford County citizens could not make up their minds about legalizing the sale of alcoholic drinks in dining and drinking establishments. Although every ward in Cadillac voted on April 7, 1908 to continue allowing liquor sales, the countywide vote defeated the initiative 2,101 to 1,766.

Missaukee and Osceola counties voted "dry" as well while Grand Traverse County voted "wet," to allow sales of alcohol.

After the two-year alcohol ban, Wexford County voted "wet" on April 4 1910 by a 241-vote margin. The Cadillac majority vote margin was 476.

Neighboring Missaukee and Osceola county residents voted to continue the ban on liquor sales. In April 1912, the county voted "dry" again by 280 votes and reversed itself once more by voting "wet" in 1914 by a margin of only 10 votes.

Although Cadillac voters supported a 1912 proposal for Women's Suffrage, the initiative was defeated in a statewide contest. It was not until 1920 that the 19th amendment to the U.S. Constitution was adopted finally giving women the right to vote.

Interestingly, it was 1924 before a woman was given a seat on a Cadillac precinct election board. Representing Wards One through Four respectively that year were Ora Moore, Lottie Mekeel, Erma LeVan and Anna J. Anderson.

In an April 1927 referendum, Cadillac voters chose "fast time" for summer hours defined as April 30 to September 3. During that period, the seasonal changing of clocks was a "local matter."

Of course, not all community improvements required ballot box approval.

City ordinances addressed most issues, some of which are rather amusing. To wit: In 1877, the city council prohibited horses, mules, cattle, swine or geese to run loose in the city. But nine years later in 1886, the council announced that cows were finally prohibited from running unattended in the city.

Also in 1877, a group of ladies started the Temperance Christian Union to combat drunkenness. In 1885, citizens were told that they must haul out of town in sealed containers waste taken from a tub, privy, drain, etc. and in 1887 the city council prohibited throwing any substance whatsoever in the lakes or the Clam River.

In 1889, a three-cent bounty on English sparrows had little boys shooting birds with toy guns and five years later a steam whistle blew at 8 p.m. every night to remind children to be off the streets at that time. Cadillac was the only town on the racing circuit that banned gambling in 1892.

Cadillac purchased four voting machines in September 1906 by using money saved from discontinuing paper ballots. (The museum is in possession of one of the machines but it is not yet prepared for display.)

Fred W. Green, Cadillac High School 1890 graduate, served as Michigan's governor from 1927 to 1931. Known as the "Good Roads" governor, he introduced the yellow roadway "no passing" line that is now used the world over.

TIMBER TOWN TALES

CADILLAC REINVENTS ITSELF

The St. John's Table Company, c. 1920's

The white pines that dominated the rolling hills of Wexford and surrounding counties drew George Mitchell and his colleagues to the eastern shore of Little Clam Lake in 1871.

By 1900 most of those towering trees had been harvested. Would Cadillac now become a "boom to bust" town like many that generated wealth quickly only to be left in shambles as the rich people fled with their money?

Absolutely not. Cadillac responded with a profound optimism and an intelligent plan. During the first 12 years of the 20th Century, a new GR & I Railroad depot, the city hall, and an opera house were built. The Carnegie library, Cadillac Boat Club, Mercy Hospital and YMCA were erected. The high school was doubled in size and a county court house was built. The Elks Temple and a new Ann Arbor Railroad depot appeared.

Most community leaders remained and new

TIMBER TOWN TALES

Cummer-Diggins and Cobbs & Mitchell office buildings occupied Mitchell Street sites. Magnificent homes were constructed in the Historical District. Mitchell Street was paved.

The seeds for the explosive burst of energy were first planted as early as the late 1880s when local industrialists contributed funds for Ann Arbor Railroad service. In January 1889 a group of leading citizens formed the Business and Professional Men's Organization to promote conventions and organize downstate tourist excursions.

That organization became the Cadillac Commercial Club (CCC) in 1899. They convinced the city to enforce fishing laws and hire a warden to control the killing of game animals. They subsidized the Odd Fellows convention and other groups who came to town.

In 1901, the CCC offered a $5,000 financial incentive if the Oviatt Manufacturing Company would move their operation to Cadillac. The incentive would "be considered a gift after the company had paid $100,000 in wages." The CCC, confident that more companies would transfer operations to Cadillac if "bonus" funds were offered, convinced the City Council to include a ballot proposition to approve $35,000 to attract industries. They also petitioned the legislature to change the names of the two Clam lakes to Lake Cadillac and Lake Mitchell.

The CCC was reorganized in February 1903 as the Cadillac Board of Trade (CBT.) The articles of the CBT are unambiguous:

" ... to encourage immigration, secure all kinds of manufacturing enterprises, ... to foster, protect and advance the commercial, manufacturing, and municipal interests of the city of Cadillac and make known the advantages of Cadillac as a manufacturing center and Wexford and adjoining counties as desirable farming country."

The promotions depended on community leaders who volunteered their time and money. City expenditures provided for publications, brochures, postage, travel and, later, subsidies to attract business and industry.

One of the first projects of the CBT was a $12,000 gift to "secure" the Union Collar Co. on River Street. They enlarged the structure that was later occupied by Goshen Shirt Co., Manistee Garment Co., Fashion Industries, Weber-Ashworth Retail Furniture Store, American Legion Hall, Kick-Away Garment Co., and, eventually, the Mitchell-Bentley Co.

In 1906, the St John's Table Co. was given a $5,300 site and a $20,000 bonus to move to Cadillac from St. Johns. The CBT secured $28,500 from the city to fund the move. In 1908 the CBT purchased a site for the Cadillac Turpentine Co. and in 1910 land was gifted for the Mitchell-Diggins Iron Co. to make high-grade pig iron using charcoal from the local chemical plants. That transaction led to the Cadillac Malleable Iron plant.

The local leadership agreed to raise $75,000 through stock options to bring the Otsego Chair Co. to Cadillac in 1910, where it operated in the city for generations.

In 1912, Mr. Diggins and Mr. Wilcox contributed half of the funding with the city providing the other half for the purchase of 24 acres from the Alexander farm for what would become Diggins Park. The Cummer family donated a water tower site of six acres of adjoining land. Over the years, the park became a major destination for young and old alike as a ski-slope, sledding area, hockey and ice-skating rinks and, more recently, tennis courts.

The CBT was dissolved in May 1916. On July 1, 1916, the Cadillac Chamber of Commerce was organized with Perry F. Powers as president and Edward Brehm as a fulltime secretary.

Tax incentives have replaced "bonuses" as a means to attract new business and industry to our town. Our forefathers demonstrated how the private sector and the political structure, working together, noticeably increased the economic strength of a community. That tradition has continued to serve us well.

TIMBER TOWN TALES

RELIGION WAS A PRIORITY

J.J. Cornish of the Reorganized Church of Jesus Christ of Latter Day Saints is shown baptizing Guy Hartnell near the Lake Cadillac shore at Kenwood Park on August 8, 1909.

The Episcopal Church conducted the first organized church activity in the Clam Lake area in 1871, the year the village was founded.

The Episcopal Diocese sent Rev. Peter Alquist to the Village of Clam Lake for what was termed, "a Mission to the Swedes." Many of the new settlers were persuaded by Rev. Dr. Josiah P. Tustin to come to Michigan from Sweden to work on the Grand Rapids and Indiana Railroad. (A previous story described the Swedish language religious groups that were organized during the first few years. They included the Swedish Evangelical Mission, Swedish Baptist, and Emmanuel Lutheran churches.)

TIMBER TOWN TALES

Most of the first churches established in Clam Lake had their origins in the United Kingdom. The family names of Wexford County's early non-Native American inhabitants were predominately of English, Scottish and Irish, as well as Swedish origins. There were also sizable numbers of Canadian, German, Dutch, Finnish, and Norwegian nationals.

Many worship venues were used before and during church construction.

The Presbyterians held their initial services in front of Clam Lake's first hotel, the Mason House, using a pine stump as a pulpit. Later, their services were conducted in a hall over a saloon, where "the keeper closed during the hour of the service, shooed his customers upstairs, but opened to accommodate them as they came down again."

The bell for the Methodist Church was installed that summer to remind people when to go to church and to remind others that they ought to do so.

It was reported that a "Mr. Badger would occupy the Presbyterian pulpit Sunday morning and the Methodist pulpit in the evening." George Mitchell donated church building lots for the Presbyterian and Methodists societies. Construction of both of those churches was started in late spring 1873.

The First Baptist Church was organized in 1876. Their first building, 31-feet by 51-feet structure, was erected in 1883 on the site they now occupy. During summers from 1904 to 1908 services were conducted at the Baptist Assembly located between the lakes.

In 1882, Dr. Charles H. Beal was sent to Cadillac by the superintendent of the Congregational Churches of Michigan to deliver a sermon. He was so well liked by those who heard him, that the village leaders contributed funds so he could move here from Manistee. John Mosser, manager of the original opera house near the lakeshore offered his facility for services "free of expense."

The church was organized in 1883 and a building was completed on its present site in December of that year.

TIMBER TOWN TALES

The true date of the "founding of the parish" of St. Ann's is unknown although as part of his mission a visiting priest from Reed City signed church records of 1883 and 1884 events. The first resident pastor was assumed to be Father L. Baroux, a Cadillac resident and an Indian missionary. Interestingly, Father Alexander Zugelder, on his way to make his headquarters in Reed City, apparently fell asleep on the train and continued on to Cadillac where he "decided that he would work out of that lumbering town on the twin lakes."

In 1900 a brick replacement church was built at the south end of Oak Street and eight years later a school was erected on the same site.

The Church of Christ (Disciples) was organized in 1905, although services were held as early as 1894 in a vacant store between Stimson and East Chapin streets. Christian Science interest emerged in 1895 when a woman seriously ill with tuberculosis was "given help" by the Society. Their meetings were first held on the second floor of the State Bank building.

Recognizing a need for a house of worship on the west side of town, legendary Dr. John Leeson bought the property and raised funds for the People's Methodist Church. The Seventh-Day Adventist Sabbath School, first organized in 1913, hosted the North Michigan Conference of the Adventists at the fairgrounds for five years.

TIMBER TOWN TALES

FIRE WAS AN EVER PRESENT DANGER

This fire destroyed several buildings on Mitchell Street between East Cass and East Harris streets in fall 1896. On the left is the Russell House Hotel. The tall structure in the center is the fire hose-drying tower on East Cass Street.

In September 1873, a fire that started in a Mitchell Street business swept southeasterly across and up East Harris Street "leaving no ruins on which to gaze."

That incident was a wake-up call. Within a few months, money had been raised to purchase water buckets and create a hook and ladder team. It was soon recognized that a large community fire-fighting force was

TIMBER TOWN TALES

essential to maintain the public safety.

In 1877 the Haynes Planing mill on West Chapin Street was destroyed by fire. Later that year, a Sunday fire on Mitchell Street "consumed everything between Harris and Mason streets."

City leaders estimated that the destruction of those fires cost a "sum eight times greater" than the city had previously requested to furnish an ample supply of lake water. Mills owned by J. W. Cobbs and Green & Bond were fire protected by the installation of steam driven pumps with pipe and hose connections on every floor as well as the roofs of the buildings.

The city sent teams to Grand Rapids in October 1877 to learn about brick and stone building construction. Brick masons were soon reported to be "kings nowadays in Cadillac." Because stone was difficult to procure, J. Cummer and Son experimented by making the foundations with concrete, water, lime, and gravel.

H. N. Green laid the first city water distribution system in 1878. Wooden logs were sawed lengthwise, hollowed out, and rejoined with metal straps leaving a six-inch diameter core

Arson was suspected when Cadillac High School was destroyed by fire in March 1884. When the replacement school burned in 1889, a brick structure was erected that existed until the 1970s.

Fires destroyed the Westover Brewery and an ice storage house. Later in 1884, Cadillac purchased new hook and ladder carts. By that time, there were three organized firefighting companies, four miles of mains and 3,000 feet of hose to fight fires. Also included were two additional hose carts and three sets of runners for winter use. There were 56 fire buckets, nine pair of rubber boots, 31 rubber coats, and four brass and two spray hose nozzles.

The city did not own teams of horses until several years later.

When the Cummer and Sons mill sounded their fire call whistle, local teamsters with horses and carts emerged from various locations and raced to the hose house located on the 100 block of East Cass Street, hoping to be among the first arrivals. After the early arriving teams were loaded with water and equipment they raced to the fire scene leaving the late arrivals with empty carts. It was the pedestrian's responsibility to avoid the running teams.

To save time rigging horses, fires in the Mitchell Street business district would be fought by men rushing from their workplaces and homes to the hose house. There they strapped on harnesses and pulled carts with six-foot diameter wheels and lengthy hoses to attach to fire hydrants.

Hose cart pulling competitions between communities were frequent.

During the summer of 1889, the Vigilant Hose Company of Cadillac won the $50 prize at Clare when they laid 300 feet of hose on a 40-rod course in 44 seconds.

In August 1892, the Cadillac Water Company owned by W. W. Cummer, installed 58 new fire hydrants throughout the city. The following year he replaced the wooden mains with 12-inch diameter iron pipes. Altogether, Cummer laid more than 10 miles of main that yielded a consumption of about a million and a quarter gallons of water daily. Cummer constructed a large water standpipe on what is now Diggins Park. By February 1894, Cadillac had 60 firefighters, two hose companies, and a very good hook and ladder company.

Fighting fires was dangerous work. In May 1893, on a dry windy day, a fire fueled by slashing from cut timbers at the Louis Sands camp in Missaukee County resulted in an uncontrollable fire that killed 10 lumberjacks.

A TOUGH AND FORGIVING LAKE

The steamboat, Westover, was the largest of several boats that transported well-dressed passengers for picnics, berry picking, and hiking in the parks and wooded areas of both lakes.

When George Mitchell convinced the Grand Rapids and Indiana Railroad Company to lay tracks on the east shore of Little Clam Lake rather than between the two lakes, he profoundly influenced the lives of generations of residents and visitors.

Since then, our ever-resilient body of water has fought off many abuses including factory pollution, careless sewage management, chemically soaked logs, over fishing and more. Yet it remains a strong, vibrant waterway that has brought pleasure and enjoyment to countless thousands.

Our little lake gets strength from its big brother to

the west. The vast wetlands around Lake Mitchell and parts of Lake Cadillac provide a continuous cleansing flow of water to the Clam River outlet resulting in a complete exchange of its water in about a year's time. Most Michigan lakes will require more than 10 years to flush their waters. Although tannin from the pine flora leaves a brownish tint to the water, its constant flow carries away large amounts of undesirable organisms making the lake less contaminated than most.

We know that the Hopewell Indians (Mound Builders) arrived in the lake area around 500 B.C.E. (BC.) More recent tribes of the Woodland Cultures (Ojibway, Ottawa and Potawatomi) most likely resided on the shores of our lakes for hundreds of years before the Europeans arrived.

It was reported as early as 1872 that our "lakes abound with excellent varieties of fish." There were many reports of 15 to 20 pound pickerel catches. Even then netting fish during spawning was considered "outrageous and spoils the sport." In March 1891, a 25-pound, 48-inch pickerel was declared the largest fish ever caught in Little Clam Lake.

In 1886, the State Fish Commission stocked the Little Clam Lake with silver eels and the Clam River with speckled trout. In May 1890, more than a million wall-eyed pike were planted. Two years later four million wall-eyed-pike were planted in Big Clam Lake. It was reported that the "wall-eyes" seemed to adapt well to these waters. Fifty-thousand salmon trout were planted but there was no indication that they survived.

By summer 1873, tourists were already arriving in the Village of Clam Lake. A steam-propelled tugboat loaded with people pulled the 20-feet by 50-feet scow, Grapevine, to picnic grounds on the north and west shores of the lake. The Grapevine, later labeled "The Belle," was equipped with a covering and dressing room and the passengers enjoyed food, drink and music on the cruise.

The cruiser Fannie Hayes took a group to the canal area for a "ramble in the woods" and another ride on the water to Graham's mill where the guests boarded a Shay locomotive for a ride among the tall pines.

In 1884, an excursion train with 600 tourists arrived from Grand Rapids for boat rides and a ball game. Later Dr. Carroll E. Miller transported 100 friends and a band on two steamers to Idlewild Park at the canal. Cadillac was becoming a serious tourist destination and the community benefitted greatly from the financial and cultural impact the visitors had on the community.

Because of considerable fluctuations of lake levels, the City Council decided to have a dam constructed on the Clam River in August 1893.

In February 1903 the Commercial club petitioned the state legislature to change the names of Big and Little Clam lakes to something more "euphonious" (sweet sounding.) A naming contest was held and prizes of $2 for each of the selected names were offered. George and Arthur Law won the prize for submitting Lake Mitchell and Mrs. Charles Donnelly for suggesting Lake Cadillac.

A concrete road around Lake Cadillac was completed in July 1916. Drivers were requested to circle the lake counter-clockwise to avoid head-on collisions.

One September morning in 1946, my parents dropped me off at my college dormitory to begin my freshman year. Noticing that the otherwise pleasant town lacked both hills and a lake, I asked them, "What do kids do for fun in this town." Obviously struggling with an answer, Mom's serious response was something like, "They probably have swing sets and seesaws at their school's playgrounds."

By the end of the first week I was homesick for the waters and hills of Cadillac.

THE YANKS ARE COMING

Cadillac celebrates the "war to end all wars."

On April 6, 1917, the United States entered World War I to assist the British and French military forces in suppressing Germany's reckless expansionism in Europe.

Three weeks later, Ray E. Bostick of Manton, Wexford County's prosecuting attorney, enlisted in the Army. On August 1, 1918, Lieutenant Bostick was killed in action at Chateau Thierry, France, becoming one of 28 warriors from Wexford County killed in action during World War I.

It has been written that that crucial battle "changed the nature of the war from an allied defensive to an allied offensive."

With its experienced management and labor force, Wexford County wasted no time in committing its industrial and other community strengths to a greater cause. A month after the war declaration, the Cummer

TIMBER TOWN TALES

Manufacturing Company assigned its entire workforce to make 1,500 ammunition boxes a week for the military.

Before the summer was over, the Cadillac Cabinet Company began making six thousand 7½-feet-by-2-feet mess (dining) tables for the Army. The tables were to be made of Michigan hardwood.

The company later received orders to make rifles and side arms repair chests. Their workforce was on site "day and night."

By June 5th, 1,748 men from the county had registered for the draft. On the July 20 draft lottery, number 258, Henning Hedlund of Clam Lake Township, was drawn.

In September a community rally and parade was staged as a demonstration of community solidarity and a salute to the men who were in the first group to be drafted. By September 1918 all men between ages 18 and 45 were required to register for draft.

More than the area's industrial strength was unleashed to support the war effort. Because of the war more than 800 women and girls were employed in Cadillac. The women knitters of the Red Cross Auxiliary were assigned a quota of 285 sweaters to send to Army camps. Later they had orders for 3,460 pairs of socks for the military. The Auxiliary had only two knitting machines.

Several churches created flags with the names of men and women who were serving in the military. St. Ann's had 36 names and the Swedish Lutherans had 28 on their flags.

Wexford County citizens consistently exceeded their targets for purchasing Liberty bonds and War Savings stamps, raising hundreds of thousands of dollars.

After 19 months of fierce fighting, the "war to end all wars" was over. The German leader Kaiser Wilhelm had fled to Holland.

The Cadillac victory celebration parade extended from Chapin Street to the Clam River and almost back to the starting point.

On November 19 Harry Haveman of Falmouth,

recovering from a gas attack at Chateau Thierry, became the first area soldier to return home.

The American Legion Post 94 was established in Cadillac on August 25, 1919 and named in honor of the war hero from Manton, Lieutenant Ray Bostick. Morton Van Meter, who served as the area's highest ranked officer, was named Post Commander.

On May 24, 1924 a new Legion burial plot for war veterans was dedicated at Maple Hill Cemetery and in 1930 the mothers of Lieutenant Bostick and Sergeant Thomas Lamont of Yuma visited their sons' graves at a U.S. military cemetery in France.

Legendary songwriter George M. Cohen was on a train that April 6, 1917 when the news broke that the U.S. had entered the war. He began humming a tune and soon put lyrics to his melody. In a short time he had created, "Over There," a most inspiring wartime song. His creation profoundly captures the unselfish spirit of Americans. Following is the chorus from "Over There."

> *"Over there, over there!*
> *Send the word, send the word over there~*
> *That the Yanks are coming,*
> *The Yanks are coming,*
> *The drums rum-tumming everywhere*
> *So prepare, say a prayer!*
> *Send the word, send the word to beware!*
> *We'll be over, we're coming over,*
> *And we won't come back till it's over*
> *Over there."*

http://history1900s.about.com/od/1910s/a/overtheresong.htm

As teenagers during World War II we sang that song proudly.

MOTOR CITY NORTH

Charles Foster is driving his truck, the first built by the Acme Company. The Foster Brothers owned a moving and coal delivery business in Cadillac for many years.

Walter A. Kysor, a Cadillac industrialist, met with the Cadillac Board of Trade on August 5, 1915 to discuss his plan to manufacture trucks in his home town. Kysor was a partner in the Cadillac Machine Co., organized in 1901. On Sept. 1, 1915, with the support of the board, he organized the Cadillac Truck Company with a "capitalization of $100,000 approved." On Dec. 2, the Cadillac Motor Car Company in Detroit told Kysor to stop using the term "Cadillac" for his vehicles.

Kysor organized his company as mostly an

TIMBER TOWN TALES

assembly operation, using a highly successful Alma, Michigan company as his model.

The Charles J. Foster Storage and Crating Company purchased the first-made Acme truck on Dec. 15, 1915. That truck was equipped with floor-mounted shift and brake levers that were operated by the driver's hand.

In 1917, under the title, Acme Truck Company, a large, modern structure was constructed on Haynes Street (now the AAR Systems facility.) Among their first products was a fire truck that gave Cadillac its first motorized firefighting equipment. Acme-made fire trucks were in use in Cadillac until the 1940s.

In the mid-1920s, after much research, Acme made several buses that featured "comfort, rapid transportation, and enjoyable travel." To make them less prone to rollovers, the height was capped at 79½ inches. A signal light was installed on the dash to advise the driver if any of the doors were open. Other features packaged by industrial genius Walter Kysor included a large, one-piece windshield, extra large headlights, a spotlight and a windshield cleaner. Passengers could lower their windows and large ventilators were installed on the roof for a comfortable airflow. Special space was provided for luggage.

Although refuted by some, Acme claimed that the bus averaged 14 miles per gallon of gas and 75 miles on a quart of oil. The bus held 14 to 16 passengers and cruised at 45 to 50 miles per hour. The Acme-built body was made of oak or white ash wood. The motor, a Continental Red Seal, was manufactured elsewhere. A 16-passenger bus that served several communities between Traverse City and Howard City was purchased for $6,545.

During the last quarter of 1921, Acme shipped 100 trucks. A dealership in Saskatchewan, Manitoba was opened with a start-up inventory of 100 trucks in 1928. Both the Acme Truck Co. and C. Z. Hinkley built experimental snowplows in 1924. In 1929 Acme built a "mobile cottage" for a New Jersey man.

TIMBER TOWN TALES

During the 1920s, Acme trucks moved about 145 houses to Cadillac from Jennings. The powerful trucks also transported churches and other buildings weighing up to 40 tons.

In 1924, Walter Kysor left his truck operation to set up another company in Allegan where he invented a combination heater and muffler for bus and taxicab manufacturers. He returned to his hometown in 1927 and established the Kysor Heater Company on Haynes Street where he developed and made thermostatic controls that could regulate heat within two or three degrees of a set point.

Acme faced serious financial problems caused by the onset of the Great Depression in 1929. While in receivership, Acme was purchased by some of the company's major creditors. Encouraged by some "good orders," operations resumed for a brief period in 1931 but the company was finally disbanded in 1932.

Over the next 40 years the Kysor enterprise designed and manufactured hot water heaters and air operated automatic shutters for heavy equipment, including rail cars. At one time Kysor shutters were used on 95 percent of all revenue buses in the U.S. Many other vehicle heating and cooling products were developed and made by the company.

By 1955, the Kysor Industrial Corporation expanded their local plant to 80,000 square feet and employed 300 men and women. By the late 1960s, the company employed 2,700 in 19 manufacturing plants in the U.S. and Canada. Kysor products were sold to five affiliated foreign companies in Europe, and one each in Australia, Japan and Mexico.

Cadillac's industrial strength was once again on display for the world to notice.

THE 1920's WAS AN ERA OF CHANGE

A 1920s view of the Drury Block on the East side of Mitchell Street between East Harris and Beech streets. The large Masonic Temple building can be seen in the next block.

No history of Wexford County would be complete without some words about that flamboyant decade following our soldiers' victorious return home from World War I.

The title of a song published in 1919 sets the tone: "How Ya Gonna Keep 'Em Down on the Farm After They've Seen Paree?" with such colorful lyrics as: "They'll never want to see a rake or a plow; And who the deuce can parleyvous a cow?"

Two very important constitutional amendments contributed to a dramatic period of change in our social structure and behaviors. The 18th Amendment (1919) made it illegal to make or sell any intoxicating beverage with a 0.5 percent or higher alcoholic content (although it was not illegal to drink alcohol) and the 19th Amendment (1920) that finally gave women the right to vote.

The 1920s began with the Chamber of Commerce giving serious attention to promoting Cadillac as a resort destination. In August 1920 the Cadillac Rotary Club was chartered with 19 members and in December Mrs. W. W. Mitchell purchased and donated to the State Park Commission the large tract of wooded land between the lakes.

It was the age of jazz, flappers, Al Capone, low priced cars (some called them "bedrooms on wheels,") home appliances, ready-made clothes, the Ku Klux Klan, migrations of southern workers to northern factories and farmers to urban centers, and a very small number of young women taking advantage of their new-found "freedoms" to smoke, drink alcohol, wear short skirts, and dance the Charleston.

Some local girls purchased knickers, but few wore them in public other than on golf courses. In Traverse City, the chief of police was ordered to "arrest any woman appearing in public garbed in 'male attire.'" That edict was soon rescinded.

Because Wexford County had voted "dry" before the 18th Amendment was enacted, prohibition had little noticeable impact on Cadillac; however, it was reported by residents of that era that a dozen or more illegal sellers of alcohol operated "almost openly." Throughout the 1920s, prohibition cases "clogged" Wexford County court dockets as bootleggers did a flourishing business here. In October 1924 it was reported that the "county jail and facilities were strained."

In 1921 a beach was developed at Kenwood Park (Community Beach) and a road north from the canal along the Lake Mitchell shoreline was improved providing access to many more acres of lake frontage.

Even though the tree harvest industry was in significant decline, the creative genius of local

TIMBER TOWN TALES

manufacturers kept the carloads of products with "Made in Cadillac" labels moving to foreign and domestic markets. Case in point: C. A. Saunders reported to the Exchange Club that local industries produce as many chemicals from wood as the combined output of those products from England, Sweden, Japan, and France.

During the winter of 1922, radio broadcasts were first heard in Cadillac. A new ordinance was passed increasing the downtown speed limit from 10 to 15 miles per hour and parking in the center of Mitchell Street was extended to North Street.

On February 22, 1922, the worst ice storm in the area's history immobilized the community for two weeks. Most trees were damaged, trains could not navigate because of several inches of ice on the tracks, and the city was left without electrical power.

A "last call" for houses to be moved to Cadillac from Jennings was issued in October 1923 as guardrails had to be installed at the Clam River Bridge. About 145 Jennings houses were transported to town on Acme trucks that were made in Cadillac. The five-ton trucks were capable of hauling 40-ton structures. One large house was "cut right in two" with each part brought to Cadillac separately.

Joe Karcher, with his powerful Acme truck and large trailer, moved buildings from Alma to Mt. Pleasant and from Raco in the Upper Peninsula to Sault Ste. Marie.

Snowstorms in 1925 led to the closure of the road to Tustin. A group of Cadillac men armed with shovels opened it up for traffic. Participating in that snow removal were Walter Kelly, Freeman and George Hemp, Arthur Finstrom, Clyde Cuddleback, Stanley Heustis, George Crawford, and L. B. Donnelly. After two days drifting snow once again closed the road.

I suspect that Cadillac High School's traditionally excellent English teachers were somewhat exasperated over these popular song titles of 1923; *"Yes, We Have No Bananas"* and *"It Ain't Gonna Rain No More."*

A VACATION DESTINATION PART ONE

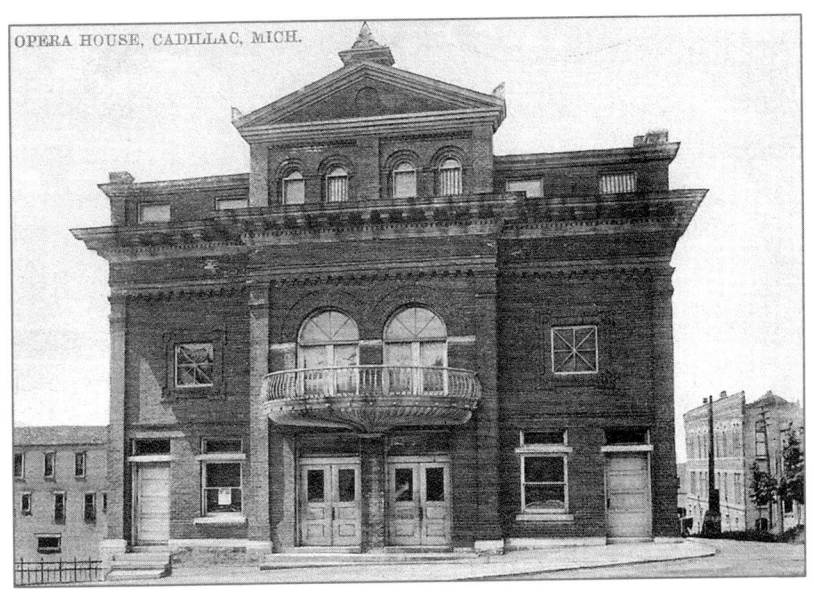

OPERA HOUSE, CADILLAC, MICH.

The 700-seat Opera House, located on the southwest corner of Beech and Shelby streets facing east, was constructed in 1901. It was destroyed by a windstorm in 1930.

During May 1873, less than a year after the Village of Clam Lake was platted, local entrepreneurs began unleashing their creative profit-making instincts. With two beautiful lakes, countless acres of prime white pine trees, rail service and a progressive new community, the area would soon attract folks seeking adventure and pleasure in Northern Michigan.

At that time, horse-drawn carriages could not navigate the dense forests that surrounded the lakes and the village. Thus the question became, "How can we use the lakes to make money?"

It was already known that the lakes were populated with excellent varieties of fish and that a plentiful supply of wild game roamed the nearby forests. By late 1872, there were four hotels in the community all doing a "prosperous" business. On February 21, 1873 the morning temperature dropped to minus 30 degrees. So began our well-deserved reputation as the "coolest" place in Michigan.

In May 1873 a tugboat was purchased by A. C. Mason who then made a flat bed scow to transport people to the north shore of Little Clam Lake and on to Idlewild, the wooded area between the lakes. Later, a competitor featured food, music and dancing on his scow.

Tourists could picnic, camp, gather berries or hike the wilderness. Three trains arrived each day bringing visitors from Grand Rapids, Kalamazoo, Traverse City and beyond.

Before the rapidly rising mills occupied all of the village's lakeshore, community founder George Mitchell set aside for the City Park the land between the Grand Rapids and Indiana Railroad depot (G.R. & I.) and the lakeshore.

As early as 1875 newspapers in other cities featured stories about the Village of Clam Lake suggesting that it was a very "social town" with music, dancing and fine dining. It was reported in 1876 that the Clam Lake cornet band had become "one of the fixed institutions of our village." (Today's visitors to the Rotary Pavilion on Monday nights during summer would agree that it was well "fixed" indeed.)

The G.R. & I. Railroad sold $16 round trip excursion tickets to Cadillac from Cincinnati during September and October 1883.

The Cadillac News editor, W. Wight Giddings urged his readers to help promote the area as a summer resort. With a little work we can be "one of the handsomest cities in Michigan." The following year the G.R. & I. brought 600 tourists to town for boat rides and a ball game.

Some projects never made it off the drawing boards.

TIMBER TOWN TALES

Gustavus O. Helbring purchased 40 acres of land between the lakes to "convert the wilderness into a modern summer resort, second to none in this state." Included in the plan was a 50-room hotel facing Big Clam Lake with two towers connected by a bridge over the Canal.

In August 1888, 500 whortleberry (huckleberry) pickers visited a marsh area in Cherry Grove Township. Later that month a special Toledo, Ann Arbor, and Northern Michigan Railroad excursion train of 14 filled coaches arrived from Ann Arbor, Owosso and other points along the route. Riders enjoyed picnics throughout the community and between the lakes. Many dined in hotels during their six-hour Cadillac outing.

Since the community's founding in 1871, steady streams of music groups, travelling road shows, lecturers, drama groups, magicians, ministerial shows and other entertainers visited Cadillac to display their talents. Most performances were held in Cummer Hall on Spruce Street and the 700-seat Opera House constructed on the southwest corner of Shelby and Beech streets in 1901.

It was occasionally reported that visitors came to the area to "uncover" Indian relics between the lakes. The ancient Hopewell Indians (mound builders) were thought to have settled in the area more than 2,000 years ago.

In October 1889 a number of local leading citizens presented a play about an old-fashioned school district meeting. The colorful description of one attendee offered the following: "It was a delirium of absurdity, a carnival of unconventionality, and a reigning of the ridiculous for two hours." (Since researching documents for these stories I have become an admirer of late 19th Century English language usage.)

TIMBER TOWN TALES

A VACATION DESTINATION PART TWO

Two fishermen from Illinois display their catch at a local sportsman's club.

While serving in the U.S. Navy at the Boca Chica Naval Air Station near Key West in summer 1950, a friend entered my work area announcing excitedly, "Your hometown is famous!"

A front-page story of the Miami Herald displayed the headline, "Cadillac Thermometer Goes Berserk."

It seems that Cadillac was the coldest place in the nation and the hottest place in Michigan on the same day. Although I don't recall my response, it should have been something like, "Yep, Cadillac is a 'cool' town populated by very warm people." (Note: With the help of a Herald staffer, I learned that the low Cadillac temperature on

TIMBER TOWN TALES

July 1, 1950 was 32 degrees and the high that day was in the 80s.)

Our town has always been a four-season destination for tourists. It was warm in July 1936 when the temperature reached a record 104-degrees and in January 1951 we received national publicity with a cool minus 43-degree reading. The area's still and moving waters, rolling hills, snow depths and unspoiled forests, have attracted sports enthusiasts, adventurers and pleasure seekers from all economic levels, ages, and out-of-doors interests. The Cadillac area, so rich in nature's bounties, benefits greatly as a four-season tourist destination.

It was reported in the summer of 1921 that "progress is remarkable in local resort areas." Road improvements in the lakes area, a new beach at Kenwood Park, and the Mitchell State Park were credited for the increased number of tourists.

While in town with a group of wholesalers during the 1920's, a proposal to make the Cadillac area a winter resort was submitted by the secretary of the Grand Rapids Association of Commerce. Two days later, Cadillac hosted another session to discuss prospects for "tourist and resort development." Attending were delegates from McBain, Marion, Houghton Lake, Lake City, Boon, LeRoy and Manton.

In July 1924, the Chamber of Commerce distributed its "first resort booklet" highlighting the area's summer "advantages."

The Oak Ridge pavilion (later "The Spot") was built in 1925 at White Sands on the north end of Lake Mitchell. At that time it was "the largest resort dance hall in the north." The following year the bandstand was constructed in the City Park.

In June 1930 the Michigan Historic and Legendary Motorcade arrived to visit Indian mounds in the area. The burial sites were located in Kenwood Park, the Cadillac Country Club grounds and Boon. The following month, 43 airplanes landed in Cadillac in their second annual air tour.

TIMBER TOWN TALES

To aid pilots, "Cadillac" was painted on the roof of the Ford garage in letters large enough to be read at a 5,000 feet altitude.

In November 1930, a contest was held to recognize the person who counted the most out-of-state license plates in Wexford and Missaukee counties during the summer months. The winner tabulated 7,380. (I assume that the "honor system" was activated.)

Later that month the 772-member Chamber of Commerce adopted the slogan "Cadillac Forward" and two years later the Chamber suggested another slogan, "Top of Michigan," to bring attention the city's location at 1,307 feet above sea level. (I like it as I have occasionally been introduced by those words.)

Cadillac received more national publicity as a cool place in February 1940 when the National Safety Council selected the north side of Lake Cadillac for driving tests. After a large section of the test area was scrapped clean by plows, it was flooded for smoothness to check tire types and chains at varying speeds.

Arguably, the area's most important vacation destination of the past 75 years, both in numbers of visitors and monetary value to the local economy, has been the Caberfae Peaks Ski and Golf Resort (formerly the Caberfae Ski Area.) Developed during the late 1930s mostly by Civilian Conservation Corps workers, it soon became one of the largest and most visited ski areas in the Midwest.

Closed from 1942 to 1945 because of the war, the ski area re-opened in the mid-1940s with ticket sales numbering up to 60,000 a season. The majority of those skiers rented rooms, dined at local restaurants, bought gas and made other purchases during their weekend outings. Credit a group of Cadillac ski enthusiasts, some big hills, a lot of snow and some refreshingly cold air for that highly successful venture that continues today.

It's likely, however, that not all visitors to Cadillac were warmly welcomed. On March 10, 1925 a funeral at Maple Hill Cemetery arranged by the Ku Klux Klan was held for a Sherman Klansman. Attending were about 25 Klansmen adorned in their robes.

TIMBER TOWN TALES

LIVING AND GIVING DURING THE GREAT DEPRESSION

Depression-era gardens like this one on West Mason Street were scattered throughout the community to grow food for the school hot lunch program.

When the stock market went into its tailspin on October 29, 1929, the impact was felt immediately as banks closed and most factories reduced or ceased operations. The "Roaring Twenties" were over. The Great Depression very quickly changed the way we would live for the next dozen years.

Adversity often brings out the best in people. While our country was experiencing the most severe financial crisis in its history, citizens worked closely with the political leadership to ensure that everybody had an adequate supply of food and a roof over their heads.

TIMBER TOWN TALES

Federal relief programs would not be in place for many months. Wexford and surrounding counties were forced to find ways to meet the needs of their residents. The salary of teachers and others were paid in locally prepared scrip (temporary paper currency) as very little money was in circulation. They would use the scrip to pay their taxes while retail stores accepted the scrip to pay their taxes. Teachers voted to have their salaries cut to avoid the dismissal of fellow faculty members.

The Cadillac Welfare Union was organized in 1932 to collect and distribute food and fuel to those most in need. In October 1932, R. J. Teeter donated his $300 state awarded bonus to the Union and a benefit party at the St. Johns Table factory, attended by 800 people, raised another $205. Local members of the American Legion implemented the National War on Depression by selecting A. L. Burridge and Tom Miller to coordinate Cadillac's participation in the initiative. Besides supporting the Welfare Union in numerous ways, Legion members assisted unemployed men seeking work in the community.

Large containers labeled "Bounty Barrels" were placed near grocery store exits for departing customers to contribute a can of soup, a bag of flour, or a box of cereal, to be distributed to needy families by the store's staff. Boy Scouts collected used clothing from area households for distribution to the poor. A Northern Michigan rabbit hunt was held that yielded 800 pounds of meat.

Untold gallons of homemade soup, made primarily from home vegetable gardens and personal stocks of canned goods, were donated to schools so children could enjoy warm nutritious lunches. During the summer 1932, Cadillac High School principal George Mills and the school's football team planted a large vegetable garden to help supply school lunch programs. The Cadillac Club and the Exchange Club were among the many organizations that sponsored welfare gardens. State PTA officials were "enthusiastic" to learn that Cadillac received national recognition for its volunteer-driven school hot lunch program.

By 1934, several federal programs were in place to assist those with little or no income. Over half of the Wexford County residents were receiving full or partial support from public funds. At least eleven Federal government agencies organized to bring relief to the nation's families, operated in the Cadillac area. Forty women of the Helping Hand Society of the Swedish Baptist Church made clothing from government-donated cloth. They also repaired shoes. The Red Cross contributed 6,800 yards of cotton cloth.

The National Relief Administration sent to Cadillac in January 1934 six tons of pork and three tons of beans. Over 3,700 pounds of cooked beef were sent the following month. The NRA later sent by rail a carload each of grapefruit and oranges. The Works Progress Administration provided 21,802 "articles of clothing" and 100 tons of food in 1937. The Federal Emergency Relief Administration donated 10,977 cans of fruits and vegetables in 1937

One might assume that because of the high level of local volunteer participation during the depression Wexford County residents suffered less than those of many if not most communities.

Interestingly, among the "Songs of the Year" introduced in 1932 were *"Happy Days Are here Again"* and *"Brother, Can You Spare a Dime."*

THE CIVILIAN CONSERVATION CORPS

Winter Play at Caberfae — Cadillac, Michigan

Caberfae skiers are transported up the hill by a rope tow. The 102 foot Caberfae Hill Fire Tower can be seen to the right of the tow behind the trees, circa 1940s.

The work of the Civilian Conservation Corps (CCC) has enriched the lives of Wexford County residents and visitors for 80 years. That Great Depression era relief agency, funded by the federal government, was created to provide employment on public forestlands for "boys and men." It was only 37 days after his March 4, 1933 inauguration that President Franklin D. Roosevelt launched the nine-year project to restore the country's forests.

An excellent description of the CCC can be found on a Michigan State University Website at http://web2.geo.msu.edu/geogmich/ccc.html/ The MSU report reveals that there were 59 CCC camps in Michigan

TIMBER TOWN TALES

and about 11,800 resident workers. Ninety percent of the candidates for the program had to be between the ages of 17 and 23.

The program was set up by the military and many features of a U.S. Army camp were implemented, although there were no military exercises. The selectees had to be in good health, strong, and within specified weight and height ranges. They were issued clothing consisting primarily of out-of-date military dress and work clothes, shoes, a cot and mattress, and toiletries. Of their $30 monthly wage, $25 had to be sent home to their families.

After the 8 a.m. to 4 p.m. workday, the men would participate in various recreational activities. Some would enroll in classes. They could visit area towns as long as they returned to camp by the 10 p.m. curfew. They were fed well and received proper medical attention when ill or injured.

The MSU report included the thoughts of one mother who suggested that, "the boys are safe there. They are young and inexperienced and need someone reliable to teach them and I think the discipline and strictness are what they need now in their teenage period."

Most of the CCC camps in Wexford County were located on cut over land returned to the government by the lumber barons and the defaulted properties that were issued under the Homestead Act of 1862. The Manistee National Forest was created in 1938 primarily from those returned lands.

Wexford County's first CCC camp was built west of Pleasant Lake in Selma Township in 1933, the year the agency was created. The camp consisted of 15 buildings constructed by the Peterson and Westberg builders of Cadillac. After six months it was vacated and the crew was sent to the Upper Peninsula. It was re-occupied in October 1934 by a new group of 225 "boys."

In the meantime a camp at Harrietta "for 200 colored youth" was established and in 1935 Camp Axin was built west of Cadillac on Highway M-55 between Hoxeyville and Caberfae. The Harrietta and Hoxeyville crews won tree-planting contests involving a dozen CCC camps. It was reported that the Harrietta men planted a record 123,525 trees in seven hours.

Wexford County camps were assigned a wide variety of projects that included tree plantings, fire tower construction, trout and wildlife surveys, flood controls, and the construction of forest trails, roads, picnic, and recreation sites. In May 1937 the CCC saved Wellston from being completely destroyed by fire. Also that year, seven trucks and 19 drivers left area CCC camps for Cairo, Illinois to provide relief for the Mississippi River flood victims.

During May 1934, CCC campers from Boon constructed the 102-foot high Caberfae fire tower. A local Chamber of Commerce committee of four, Secretary Floyd McCarthy, Charles Miltner, Dr. Greg Moore, and Ed Westberg, negotiated with U.S. Forest Service Ranger Howard Cook to prepare the Caberfae Tower hill as a ski area. A topographical survey was launched in 1936 by the CCC, which also provided the labor for clearing land for ski slopes and access roads as well as the construction of the main shelter.

A "national precedent" was set when a class of campers, ages 17 to 25, were granted eighth grade diplomas by completing requirements at three area CCC camps. The graduation ceremony was held at Manton High School in March 1937 where a State Department of Public Education official issued their diplomas. In 1939, 200 Camp Axin enrollees received educational certificates.

In February 1936, a series of powerful snowstorms paralyzed the area. The CCC campers assisted communities with snow removal until they were immobilized due to the storms.

TIMBER TOWN TALES

THE WORKS PROGRESS ADMINISTRATION

A Mitchell Systems parade vehicle with intriguing signage that reads: "Roosevelt; What Has He Done That You Would Undo?" One might find the responses interesting.

Soon after Franklin D. Roosevelt was inaugurated as president in March 1933, his administration created several federal relief agencies to reduce the widespread poverty resulting from the stock market crash of October 1929.

Following the April 1933 launch of the Civilian Conservation Corps were 10 additional federal agencies established to provide financial support for agriculture, rural electrification, child welfare, education and more.

The largest of the relief programs, introduced in

1935, was the Works Progress Administration (WPA, renamed Work Projects Administration in 1939.) Millions of men and women, mostly unskilled, were hired for construction of public buildings, roads, recreation facilities, sewage systems and other projects.

Money was also provided for the arts, education, and job training. It was felt that payment for work performed was better than public assistance as it helped workers maintain their self-respect, reinforced their work ethic, and provided them with job skills.

Cadillac, a traditional Republican Party community, was quick to embrace the socialistic-style government dole, feeling perhaps that desperate times call for desperate behaviors. Unquestionably, the area benefited greatly by the many and varied WPA projects.

On March 9, 1935, Wexford County submitted to the state an inventory of needed public works. Listed were 49 projects with a cost estimate of $1,355,296. The WPA soon provided workers for the summer farm harvest season. Schools in Selma Township and Meauwataka received support for repairs.

Also in 1935, a "large force of men" was assigned for the extension and improvements to the Cadillac sewage disposal plant, a WPA project that cost $45,383. A city vegetable garden was planted by the Garden Club along the east side of the Pennsylvania Railroad near the station to provide food for school lunches. Club president, Henry Knowlton supervised the WPA labor crew. A project at Cadillac's airport called for four clay-surfaced runways and a hanger.

In November 1935, approval was granted by the WPA for six projects to employ 565 men in Wexford County for roadwork in Liberty, Greenwood and Cherry Grove townships; the Harrietta fish hatchery, expansion of Maple Hill Cemetery and the relocation of four railroad crossings near Harrietta.

The cemetery project began in October 1937 with a $12,144 WPA donation and $581 from the cemetery board. Twenty men were assigned to work on the southeasterly expansion. At that same time it was determined that the construction of the fairgrounds grandstand with a seating capacity of 2,200, would be an $11,000 WPA-funded winter project.

A March 1938 report revealed that 70,780 ice skaters used the WPA-operated skating venues during the winter. While most, 56,000 were counted at the just-completed Diggins Park rink, others enjoyed a skate at the Cass School (the other land rink,) Little Lakes (near the cemetery by the city dump,) and the mill pond (presumably on Lake Cadillac near the Clam River.)

Included in WPA projects were the construction of new and the improvement of existing playground facilities, mostly at public school lots.

James Frisbie was appointed the WPA recreational supervisor and Virgil Meusil was given responsibility for playgrounds and beaches.

The Manton Park was improved with a crew of WPA and National Youth Administration workers.

A. L. Burridge, consulting engineer for the Road Commission, reported that Wexford County "has the largest WPA load of any county with which he works."

Road projects were planned to give the workers winter employment. For young boys the WPA supported a craft shop in the basement of the Elks Club.

The WPA sponsored a toy loan program that attracted nearly 100 youngsters who could borrow the toys "for a while." They also supplied cooks and surplus food for school hot lunch programs.

Not all unemployed men were interested in the work opportunities offered by the WPA. Returning home from Cooley School for lunch, I was sometimes greeted by two or more unshaven men in tattered clothes sitting on our back door steps with a sandwich or a bowl of soup.

Our home was less than two blocks from both railroads and hoboes, sometimes called "drifters" or the more derogatory term, "tramps," rode the rails from town to town hoping, I presume, to find an easier life somewhere. Mom never refused their always-polite request for food, although they had to imbibe outside.

They were friendly and sincerely appreciative of Mom's generosity. Some even admitted that they were "return visitors." I enjoyed brief conversations with them and was somewhat envious of their life style. They always displayed exemplary behavior.

TIMBER TOWN TALES

A CHILD OF THE GREAT DEPRESSION

Legendary educator Lynn Corwin is seen with his 1935 Cass Grade School championship basketball team. Corwin was also the first and a longtime director of the Cadillac School Camp (Camp Torenta.)

Early days in Cadillac's south end were very special to me. We passed the time by engaging in rather competitive sandlot football and softball games in the church yard, playing cowboys and Indians in Horseshoe Hollow, hiking in Brown's woods, exploring the mysteries of abandoned factories, the city dump, the gravel pits, "borrowing" rhubarb and apples from neighborhood garden lots, skiing in Devil's Kettle in the Maple Hill Cemetery, and swimming

TIMBER TOWN TALES

and fishing in Lake Cadillac down by the old sawmill and grassy dock.

When boredom set in, I would approach one of my friends homes with a loud "hey, Gary," or "Fred," or any one of several boys who lived in the neighborhood. Children then would not think of bothering the parents by knocking on the door.

Everybody's mom was a good cook and I was frequently invited in for milk and freshly baked cookies as I sought playmates.

While none of the families in our neighborhood was well off financially during those years of the Great Depression, they all seemed to get by.

Fathers, who were fortunate enough to be employed, worked 50 to 70 hours a week and mothers stayed home to manage the household and children.

Dad was very good at his trade and seemed always to have work. I can never recall being hungry because of either too little or a poor quality of food. Mom was among the several thoughtful ladies who would frequently be seen walking a covered tray of prepared food to a needy or elderly neighbor.

My winter clothing was warm and always kept clean and in good repair by Mom.

Almost every Saturday, I would have the 10 cents needed to watch the triple feature of cowboy movies at the Center Theater. Occasionally, Dad managed to treat us to a Sunday supper uptown at the Club Cafe.

During those Great Depression years my "employment" consisted of collecting and selling scrap iron, brass and copper that was found along the railways and abandoned mill yards, managing Kool-Aid stands, selling magazines, and peddling newspapers.

My two- to three-mile Grand Rapids Press route started uptown and ended out on Poplar Street (now Sunnyside Drive) with several side streets included.

While I don't recall ever missing a delivery to a customer, I was sometimes "delayed" when I accepted an invitation to play a little football with the Lectkas, a very athletic family along my route.

Each week, one dollar of my $1.19 earnings was invested in Defense Saving Stamps. My bicycle, a single speed Schwinn, was my year-around vehicle, pushing through snow and ice often at temperatures well below zero and once hitting minus 40 degrees.

Dad's constant reminder sustained me: "If you live in Cadillac," he would say, "you must either adjust to the cold, or expect to be miserable half of your life."

Never did I request nor was I ever given a ride in an automobile to carry out my paper delivery responsibility.

One time when my errant behavior brought Mom to quiet tears, my guilt feelings over the incident left me with some emotional turmoil. My remorse motivated me to visit the Johnson's Hardware store up on South Mitchell Street. I wanted to use my $1.19 weekly earnings for a gift for Mom. The clerk, obviously eager to get a rather unattractive red doughnut-shaped teapot removed from his inventory, recommended it as a nice gift for Mom.

Upon receiving the "unique" gift, tears welled up in Mom's eyes once again, albeit tears of joy. That teapot now rests in storage with an appraised value of $480.

People trusted each other. You could always find the car keys; they were in the ignition where they belonged. As far as I know, we did not have a house key. The door was always unlocked.

One day when an uncle from Detroit visited my Swedish-born grandmother on East Nelson Street, he implored her to keep her doors locked. When he returned a few weeks later, her door was locked, but the key was hanging on a nail at eye level on the outer door casing. When asked "why?" she replied perplexed, "In case someone wants to get in!"

We formed clubs frequently, but they seldom lasted more than one or two days. Democracy was alive and well on Wood Street. It just couldn't be sustained. The upside was that we all had many chances to be "leaders." If nobody elected me, I would simply form my own club and install myself as president, or general, or some such title.

The clubs seldom had a purpose. After election of the officers, a meeting site had to be created. Members gathered tarps, old stools, rope, boxes, boards, rugs, and other items from their parent's garages, which were then carted to the "office" site, typically under a tree on a vacant lot.

The first order of "business" was to select a name and representative colors for our club. Many names were taken from athletic teams such as Tigers, Wildcats, Bears, Wolverines, Spartans, and, of course, Vikings. Wimpy names, such as Cubs, Orioles, Gophers, Red Sox and Cardinals were never considered.

At our new "office," we sat and talked about sports, people, cowboy movies and the new family on the block. That evening, or the following day, the club was dissolved and the "building" materials were returned to their rightful places.

Oh, to be a kid again.

DISCIPLINE DURING THE TIMES OF TURMOIL

Located one half mile north of city limits on US-131 was Dad and Ma's Barbecue and gas station, a depression era business, c. 1930.

We sometimes hear about the numerous difficulties children faced growing up during the Great Depression and the World War II eras.

During the 1930s most families were struggling to meet their financial responsibilities. Later, our lives were consumed by the many sacrifices we made to support the war effort. Those two worldwide forces, the economy and the war, most likely helped to ameliorate some traditionally challenging conditions both parents and teachers faced as they dealt with childhood behaviors and discipline.

Because both parents were seldom employed during the depression years, moms remained home to watch over their children's activities. If you tossed a stone through a neighbor's window, you or your parents had to pay for the repair so we mostly avoided destructive behaviors. Some might say we were too poor to be "bad boys."

We took our responsibilities for the care and protection of our toys and clothing seriously as there was little money for replacements should they be lost or destroyed. Further, there were far fewer child psychologists then who suggested that parents allow their children to display their bad behaviors in any way they wished lest they grow up to be neurotic "basket cases."

During the war years, gas rationing gave parents a viable reason to deny their older children use of the family sedan. Much potentially destructive teen-age energy was released by walking across town to pick up your date, return downtown to the movie house or a dance hall, accompany her home, and trek back to your home.

Car use today gives teen-agers an exposure to many of life's temptations that are unavailable to walkers. Because we arrived at a driving age during the fuel restrictive 1940s, we didn't miss the driving culture that became so prevalent in later generations.

As I look back on my childhood, I have concluded that my parents were very good disciplinarians. I don't recall ever being spanked, grounded for days, or sent to bed without supper. I was never called a "bad boy" nor did Mom or Dad ever say that they were disappointed in my behavior.

It must have been difficult for them to curb their feelings at those times that I did disappoint them. When I exhibited unacceptable behavior, which probably happened more than occasionally, Dad would simply tell me what I did was wrong and make me promise that in the future I would think before acting. Occasionally I would be sent to my room for a short while to contemplate my inappropriate behavior.

While I don't think he ever voiced such, I always felt that his expectations of me were very high which seemed to motivate me to accept his guidance and continually strive to achieve lofty levels of good behavior.

I grew up with a dogmatic determination to not in any way disappoint my parents.

Mom, always the quiet supporter of Dad's child rearing methods, worried when I failed to appear home at an expected time.

I once told her that I was late getting home from school because I "took a shortcut."

It was true! A straight line from Cooley Grade School to our home on Wood Street bisected a small wetlands area that had all kinds of things to interest young boys. There I would enjoy the always standing water, frogs, snakes, turtles, colorful bugs, and an abandoned well.

That well proved to be a center of adventure, one that could be entered and exited with a bit of courage and athleticism, albeit a pastime that surely would be seen today as dangerous and maybe illegal. Since that episode, my parents would ask whenever I was late for a meal or an event, "Did you find another shortcut home?"

Maybe growing up during the Great Depression years helped us to adjust to adverse social and economic conditions in later years. Because we did not experience the more affluent and carefree life of the Roaring Twenties, we did not know that we were living under economical hardships.

I have since observed during many experiences in Third and Fourth World countries that people of those places seem to be happy and that they possess similar hopes and expectations for a better future for their children even though they lacked almost everything that we take for granted.

As I grew older, my parents often reminded me of the problems they faced during the 1930s. I could not comprehend how difficult it was to raise a family with so few resources and the constant lingering anxieties of unemployment.

LEADERS AND FOLLOWERS

Skaters enjoy a skate at the Standpipe Hill (later called Diggins Park) rink. Note the large number of observers of a hockey match on the far side of the rink. The "warming hut" was located near the lower right corner of the image.
c. late 1930's.

My grandson, Wes, is an excellent hockey player. His teams played before large crowds on rinks throughout Michigan, including the Joe Lewis Arena in Detroit.

His 40-game season, under the direction of three coaches, lasted from October to April. The team's webpage listed his achievements: Captain, leading scorer, and the "most valuable player" award. His team was provided with colorful, professional-looking uniforms and the best equipment. A Zamboni refreshed the ice between periods.

Wes was 9 years old at that time!

Many children these days spend their earlier years

on carefully crafted playgrounds with their spiffy uniforms and well-designed equipment, at contests organized and supervised by adults, and under the critical eyes of their cheering and sometimes complaining parents. The thrills of receiving trophies, publicity, team travel, team uniforms, and other experiences, once delayed until high school years and beyond, are now in danger of being "used up" before the child has attained the maturity to make wise decisions about his or her teen-age thrill-seeking activities. Unfortunately, some will later seek their "thrills" by engaging in self-destructing behaviors.

I often reminisce about my early years in Cadillac. During the 1930s and early 1940s, fathers typically worked six days a week while mothers managed their labor-intensive homes, leaving them and their neighbors little time for involvement in their children's playtime.

Children of the 1930s amused themselves by organizing and playing "pick-up sports" and games of all kinds. At that time there were no adult organized sport programs for young children other than those sponsored by Cadillac's six elementary schools. Tackle football sans pads or headgear, boxing, softball, ice and street hockey, and soccer were played on vacant lots, churchyards, school playgrounds, on the lake, and in open fields. In sandlot sports it was up to the participants to agree on the rules and to conduct their own officiating. It worked that way because unfair play would quickly lead to the end of the contest.

Many life lessons were learned during those games, including good sportsmanship, team play, acceptable winning and losing behaviors, and, most importantly, leadership skills. When teams were formed, the younger, smaller, or less athletically endowed boy would be the last chosen, but the contestants on both sides would usually "cut him some slack" so he could enjoy the experience.

It takes real-life experience to be a good leader as well as a good follower and we should not deny our young citizens those experiences. My generation learned fair play, honesty, team work, even a workable political process, as well as good competition with friendly adversaries. We learned ways of choosing leaders and we devised clever strategies to keep neighborhood bullies from dominating the activities. We were living evidence that children are fully capable of learning life's lessons without the constant presence of adults.

While today's youngsters enjoy the many sports activities that are generally well managed by dedicated men and women, something may be missing. Children are taught to play the game with adults present who make the rules, manage the play, and reward those players who do what they are told to do. We are producing generations of good followers but how are today's children learning the skills required of good leaders? Are we denying today's children the opportunity to learn life's important lessons by over supervising, over spending, and over programming their out-of-school activities? There are no "born leaders." Leadership is a skill learned by experience.

As I approach the later years of my life, I reflect often on the lessons I learned growing up in Cadillac. I remain convinced that my preparation to successfully manage two large office staffs and serve as president of my national professional organization began at the Cobbs Street churchyard in the 1930s.

It causes one to wonder if today's political and business leaders would demonstrate a bit more ability, creativity, and civility in the conduct of their responsibilities if they had been afforded the opportunity of adult-free playground experiences with all of its intrinsic benefits. Have you noticed that nearly all extremists are followers?

TIMBER TOWN TALES

WEXFORD COUNTY GOES TO WAR

This Honor Roll containing over 1,200 names was located on the south side of the Cobbs and Mitchell office building on East Chapin Street. A veteran's organization reported that more than 1,800 Wexford County men and women served their country during World War II.

In 1941, one of the largest motorized pleasure boat companies in the world acquired the former Mitchell Brothers Flooring facility on Wright Street in Cadillac. Soon after the December 7th Japanese attack on Pearl Harbor, the Chris Craft Boat Corporation restructured its operation and by January 1942 began making LCVP's (Landing Craft Vehicle Personnel) for the U.S. Navy. By the end of World War II in 1945, Chris Craft had made more than 2,000 of the large boats. The company was awarded the Navy "E" pennant for Excellence. Once again, Wexford County's considerable contributions to our nation's war efforts had been launched.

In March 1942 a Civil Aeronautics Patrol was organized and the Cadillac Company of Michigan State Troops was assembled with 88 area men registered. In May, the first group of Civilian Defense volunteers was created with 120 trained air raid wardens. A local Civilian Defense medical staff was organized and led by Dr. J. F. Gruber. In October, the U.S. Army asked Wexford County to create a ground observation corps to identify aircraft.

Few sparsely populated areas contributed more to the war effort than did the cluster of Wexford, Missaukee and Osceola counties. Seventy years of an innovative and highly diversified industrial base staffed by experienced workers led to a relatively smooth wartime conversion to product development and manufacturing of wood products, iron works, chemicals, vehicles, watercraft, rubber, wood alcohol, truck heating and cooling technology, furniture, fabrics, canvas and more.

At least 17 local industries received war contracts while several others supplied the contract companies. Kysor Heater provided vehicle makers with vital heating products and technology. St. John's Table Company made mess hall tables and other wood products for the army becoming one of several local factories with a 100 percent commitment to military clienteles.

The B. F. Goodrich Company created and manufactured a collapsible-type housing unit for the military and later designed and made pulsating wing deicers and brake expander tubes for warplanes. A shortage of local workers led Goodrich to open manufacturing facilities in Frankfort and Reed City.

Tricot, Inc. manufacturer of mosquito netting, converted its cotton yarn production to camouflage netting for use primarily in South Pacific war zones.

The Cadillac Fabrics Company produced canvas goods, ski mittens, tents, military caps and "bomb parachutes" of silk and rayon. Peterson and Westberg made ammunition boxes for the army.

At various times, Wexford County was the first in Michigan to reach monthly war bond quotas. Cadillac earned a pennant for scrap metal collected by averaging 162 pounds for each resident of the community.

Women and children took on major tasks to defeat our enemies. Local Red Cross volunteers made more than 54,000 surgical dressings for the military. Groups consisting mostly of school children collected 15,000 bags of milkweed used to make life jackets for airmen. The youngsters also collected 26,000 pounds of paper in one week. More than 300 War/Victory gardens were planted throughout the community.

Women became very creative managing their homes and children under strict wartime rationing regulations. Hundreds of women also took on factory employment as most of the area's men between ages 18 and 40 were serving in the military forces. They collected and delivered to their grocers the grease from their cooking oils for distribution to military and domestic users.

As a Boy Scout I camped with my troop not in a forest at the water's edge but in a Traverse City area orchard harvesting cherries. When forest fires arose, we were dismissed from high school classes, outfitted with a shovel and a tank of water, and sent into the woods to fight another kind of battle.

With war come the inevitable casualties. While several local men had been listed as "missing in action," Lt. Lawrence Baldinus of Yuma was the first reported warrior killed in action when his plane was shot down following his attack of a Japanese warship. Later that month Cadillac native Veikko Leivo was killed while serving with the U.S. Navy in the Solomon Islands. Many Wexford County men gave their lives in the service of their country during World War II.

TIMBER TOWN TALES

We looked up to those men and women of the "Greatest Generation." They were our heroes.

CADILLAC OPERA HOUSE ON SW CORNER OF SHELBY AND BEECH STREETS FACING EAST.
SKETCH BY FRED H. LAMB